SEVEN SLEEPERS **THE LOST CHRONICLES** 6

THE VICTIMS OF NIMBO

GILBERT MORRIS

MOODY PRESS
CHICAGO

ISBN: 0-8024-3672-2

1 3 5 7 9 10 8 6 4 2

Printed in the United States of America

Contents

1. Who Needs Boys?   5
2. "I Cannot Put My Trust in Females!"   15
3. Danger in the Forest   23
4. Land of the Cloud People   33
5. A Strange City   43
6. Sarah Decides   55
7. The Trail   67
8. Sarah Gets Some Help   77
9. The Priest's Decision   85
10. Bad News   95
11. The Miracle Shot   105
12. Death to the Female   117
13. Time of the New Moon   125
14. A Prince Becomes a Man   137
15. A Friend in the Darkness   145
16. A New Way   149

1
Who Needs Boys?

Sarah Collingwood was ordinarily a most mild-mannered girl. At fourteen she even seemed to have a special ability for peacemaking. Whenever any of the Seven Sleepers fell into arguments, it was Sarah who managed to step between and pour oil on the troubled waters.

But right now Sarah's eyes glinted with anger.

She was small and graceful, with large brown eyes and black hair drawn back into a ponytail. The sun had given her a nice tan. She wore a light blue shirt, a skirt of darker blue that came down below her knees, and half-boots made of soft leather.

But there was nothing soft about Sarah's voice as she yelled, "Josh, I've told you a thousand times to leave my things alone!"

Josh Adams, at fifteen, was tall and awkward and unsure of himself, especially where girls were concerned. He had known Sarah even back in OldWorld—before the earth had been practically destroyed by a nuclear war. Ever since their adventures in NuWorld had started, he'd felt that Sarah was the steadiest of all of the Sleepers.

So now, bewildered, he stared at her and stammered, "But . . . but . . . what are you talking about, Sarah?"

"I'm talking about what have you done with my bow."

"Your bow?" She had to see that he was puzzled. "I

don't know what you're talking about! I haven't touched your bow!"

"Don't tell me that! You borrowed it last week without asking permission! That means you took it again."

"I didn't think you'd mind my borrowing it last week!"

"Well, I did mind!" Sarah put her hands on her hips, and her voice rose in anger. "Haven't you ever thought that it might be more polite to ask before you take people's things?"

By now Josh was speechless. The previous week he *had* taken Sarah's bow without asking her, but she had not seemed to mind at the time. As he blinked at her in surprise, he found himself growing a little angry. He found his voice.

"Anyway, I didn't take your old bow! And that's all there is to it!" he said defiantly.

Always before, Sarah would have taken Josh at his word, but her nerves were likely tense. The Sleepers had been involved in a very difficult and dangerous assignment. It was for Goél, leader of the forces in Nu-World doing battle against the Dark Lord, who sought to enslave everyone. Josh realized that the strain of the mission had taken a toll on all of them.

She shoved her face close to his. "You have no more manners than a pig!" she said.

"A pig! You're calling me a pig?"

"That's what I said! No. You're worse than a pig. Pigs don't take people's things without asking."

"I didn't take your old bow!" Josh's nerves were also tight, and he suddenly found himself angrier than he had ever been at Sarah. "I don't have to take this! If you can't keep up with your things, don't blame me for it!"

Their voices rose as they shouted at each other. They were interrupted by a newcomer. A tall boy about their age appeared. Bob Lee Jackson, always called Reb by his friends, had light blue eyes, tow-colored hair, and a heavy Southern accent. He wore a fawn colored shirt, blue pants, and boots, but the most striking of his clothing was his high-crowned Stetson hat with a feather in its red band. He had been a rodeo rider before coming to NuWorld and probably was the strongest and toughest of the Sleepers.

"What y'all fussing about?" he asked with puzzlement in his eyes. "I could hear you a mile away. What's the shouting about?"

Sarah turned to him. "He stole my bow!"

"I didn't do any such thing!" Josh snapped. "I haven't even seen your old bow!"

Reb said, "Uh . . . isn't that it right over there, leaning against the tree?"

Sarah whirled. Sure enough, there was the bow she had accused Josh of stealing. It was a beautifully constructed weapon made of yew, and she had made it herself. It was smoothly polished and had a sixty-pound pull. Sarah was the most expert in the use of the bow of all the Sleepers, and her bow was as precious to her as Reb's cowboy hat was to him.

A moment's silence reigned, and then Sarah muttered, "I didn't see it!" She walked away without an apology, her back stiff. Picking up the bow, she disappeared into the woods that surrounded their small house.

"What's biting her?" Reb marveled. "Never heard her carry on like that before."

"She's getting impossible to work with," Josh murmured. "I don't know what's the matter with her."

"Well, mostly she's just a girl. And you know how girls are. Not nice and steady like us guys."

Josh could not hold back a smile. Reb was always cheerful. He knew also that Reb did not mean that. "I guess you're right," he said. "Have to make allowances for girls."

Dave Cooper walked into the house and went at once to the kitchen. A pot bubbled over the fire in the fireplace, and he lifted the lid and sniffed. "Smells good!" he said.

At sixteen, Dave was the oldest of the Sleepers and a good-looking boy with slightly curly brown hair and gray eyes. He reached for a spoon.

But the girl who was making bread hurried over and slapped his hand. Abbey Roberts was a pretty girl of fourteen with blue eyes and blonde hair.

"Leave that alone!"

"Hey! Don't go beating on me!" Dave protested. "I'm just hungry!"

"You'll have to wait until dinner!"

He was irritated by Abbey's shortness. "You're sure getting snippy," he said. "What's wrong with you?"

"Nothing's wrong with me!" And she began complaining.

Dave listened for a while, shocked. Then he shook his head, picked up a spoon, lifted the pot lid, and tasted the stew.

"I told you to stay out of that stew! Didn't you hear me? Have you gone deaf?"

Dave, like the other Sleepers, had not yet recovered from the trying time they had had on their recent adventure. He glared at Abbey and said, "That's probably the worst stew I've ever eaten!" It was actually very good stew, but by now Dave's temper was out of order.

"You don't have to eat it if you don't like it!"

"Men always are the best cooks, anyway."

"What are you talking about?"

"I mean back in OldWorld. When you went to a fancy restaurant, all the chefs were men. You never saw a woman chef in a fancy restaurant, did you?"

"Then you can just go to your fancy restaurant!" Abbey said shrilly. Dave held a full spoon in his hand, and she reached out and slapped it. The stew flew onto his shirt. "You can just cook for yourself if you don't like the way I do it!"

Dave glared at her and then at the stain on his shirt. "You didn't have to do that."

"You didn't have to come in here and complain about the cooking! Now, get out of the kitchen!"

Dave left at once, biting on his lip to keep from retorting. He went across the open clearing to where Jake Garfield and Wash Jones sat with their backs against a big tree.

Gregory Randolph Washington Jones was the smallest of the Sleepers. He was also the best humored. He said, "What's wrong, Dave? You look like you've been stung by a bee."

"Worse than that," Dave growled. "I've been chewed up by Abbey. What's *wrong* with her?"

Jake Garfield, a year older than Wash, was short with red hair. He grinned. "She pull you up short, Dave?"

"Yes, she did. Again. And I'm getting tired of it!" He sat down by the two boys. They had just started to talk about their past adventure when Josh came by and joined them. He had a sour look on his face, and Dave asked, "What's wrong with you, Josh?"

"It's Sarah. She accused me of stealing her old bow. I hadn't even touched it. Really bawled me out for no reason at all!"

"You know what I think?" Wash said slowly. "I think those girls are just worn out. That last assignment we had was a stem-winder!"

"It was just as hard on us as it was on them!" Dave said stubbornly.

"Yes, it was," Josh agreed. "Tell you what," he said, as if a sudden thought had come to him. "I think they need some time to themselves, and I guess maybe we do, too."

"What you got on your mind?" Jake asked.

Actually Josh had nothing on his mind. Sarah had hurt his feelings, and he thought it would teach her a lesson if she had to take care of her own things for a while. But he said, "Here's what I'd like to do. You know that stretch of woods about twenty miles from here—the one that's got the bayou on it?"

"Sure. Those are nice woods," Wash said. "What about 'em?"

"I think we ought to go on a little hunting expedition over there. Just us guys."

"You mean leave the girls behind?" Wash asked. "That might hurt their feelings."

"It's better than hurting *my* feelings all the time," Josh said. "It'll be good for them. Maybe they'll appreciate us if they have to do without us for a while."

"I think he's right," Dave promptly said.

"Well, it suits me," Jake said. "Nothing to do around here while we wait for a new mission, anyhow."

The four boys talked it over, and when Reb appeared, he too was eager. Reb was always ready to go on hunting trips, but when Josh told him about leaving the girls behind, he grinned. "I don't think they'll like that. You're not in very good favor, anyhow, Josh. You'd better think it over."

But Josh's pride was severely bruised. "Nothing to think over," he said gruffly. "I'll go tell them. We can leave in the morning."

Sarah was helping Abbey get the noon meal ready when Josh came in.

"I've decided that the guys are going out on a hunt," he told them.

Sarah looked up at him. "A hunt? Where to?"

"Over where that bayou is. About twenty miles north of here."

Actually Sarah was sorry that she had lashed out at Josh, but something about the way he looked and spoke irritated her. "What time are we leaving?" she asked.

"This is just for us guys," he said importantly.

"What do you mean, just for guys?" Abbey asked, looking surprised.

"I mean there are some dangerous beasts over there. You girls don't need to be going. It's too dangerous."

Abbey flushed, and Sarah felt her own face redden. They had been through many adventures together with Josh and the other boys. And now suddenly some place was "too dangerous."

"'Too dangerous'? Let me remind you, Josh Adams," Sarah flared up, "that I was the one who saved you from that wild boar! If I hadn't put an arrow into him, he would have killed you."

"No, he wouldn't have," Josh said.

11

He knows very well that I saved his life, Sarah thought.

"You two girls have gotten impossible to live with," he said sternly. "We're going to go away and give you some time to think. Maybe you can get into a better humor."

As soon as Josh left, Sarah slammed down a pan of biscuits on the table, jarring it. "Too dangerous! I like that!"

"Who do they think they are?" Abbey asked. She didn't care much about hunting, but likely the thought of being deliberately left out was irritating. "Boys— who needs them?"

The rest of the day was tense, for the girls would speak only in short sentences. All the boys could see that they were ruffled.

Once Wash whispered, "Why don't you break down and be generous, Josh? The trip'll be fun for them. They'll be all right."

But Josh Adams, who usually was quite amiable, was also stubborn. "No, they need time to get over whatever it is that's eating them. We'll give them a couple of days."

At dawn the next morning, when the boys got up, they found no one to cook breakfast for them. Wash did the best he could, but as they sat down to eat, he admitted, "Afraid I'm not the cook Abbey is—or Sarah."

"It's all right, Wash," Josh said. "It's good enough." Actually he was already regretting his decision. But he did not want to back down, so after breakfast he said, "All right. Let's go."

Both Sarah and Abbey heard the door slam, but it

was Sarah who said, "Well, they're gone. And good riddance." She snuggled back under the warm covers and muttered, "Boys—who needs them? We can get along without them very well."

2

"I Cannot Put
My Trust in Females!"

W ell, I hope they're enjoying themselves!"
Sarah crossed the kitchen and poked a fork into
a steak that was frying in the pan. There were two of
them, tender and juicy, and the aroma of the cooking
meat smelled good.

"I hope they're eating half-cooked meat and getting indigestion," she muttered.

Abbey entered and came to the stove. "What'd you
say, Sarah? Ooh, that looks good!"

"Yes, they're nice and tender. And we're going to
have baked potatoes with fresh butter. And I've made a
chocolate pie—Josh's favorite. But he won't get any of
it."

"What is it you were saying when I came in?"

"I was saying I hope the boys eat half-cooked meat
and get indigestion."

Abbey laughed at that. "You're really annoyed at
Josh, aren't you?"

"Shouldn't I be?"

"Oh, *I* feel a little better this morning. I was cross
enough yesterday. But I guess we were all upset and
tired, and our nerves were a bit tight."

Sarah removed the steaks and put them on individual plates. "These are done," she said. "If you'll get
the potatoes, we can eat."

The two sat down to a delicious meal.

Abbey asked at one point, "Do you miss being back in OldWorld, Sarah? You never talk much about those times anymore."

Sarah chewed thoughtfully on a small bite of steak. Finally she nodded. "I guess I do. Of course I miss my folks."

"I do, too," Abbey said sadly. "Sometimes at night I wake up and just cry about it."

"Do you do that? So do I!" Sarah exclaimed. "I wonder if any of the boys feel that way."

"They'd never tell if they did." Abbey nodded wisely. "You know how boys are. They think it's a shame to shed a tear."

It had been a beautiful day. The sun was almost down now, and its last rays came through the window as the girls talked. Sarah could hear the frogs croaking down in the small river close by. Then abruptly the noise stopped, and both girls sat a little straighter.

"Something scared those frogs," Abbey said.

Both girls rose at once and picked up their swords. There were no guns in NuWorld, only swords, spears, and bows. Fortunately, the Sleepers had become fairly expert in all of them, for they were in a world of dangerous beasts never seen before on the earth. The nuclear war had done strange things to genetics. In NuWorld there were even creatures much like dragons.

Sarah opened the door and stepped outside. She saw two figures emerge from the woods, and she focused on them sharply. She was always suspicious of strangers, because there was special danger in this world for the followers of Goél.

"Who is it, Sarah?" Abbey asked from behind her.

Sarah did not answer for a moment, and then she cried out, "Goél!"

The two figures came forward at once. The taller was wearing a light gray robe with a hood over his head. Now he pushed it back. His features were strong, and most noticeable were the eyes. They seemed to glow, and their directness would have startled many people.

"Well, daughter, I'm glad to have found you." He took Sarah's hands for a moment, and she felt the confidence that always came with meeting Goél. Then he turned to greet Abbey. "Abigail, you're looking very well indeed!"

Abbey blushed. Everyone, including Goél, was aware that she thought too much of her appearance. She'd had to learn that outward beauty was not as important as what lay in the heart. However, she was obviously glad to see him.

He took both her hands in one of his and squeezed them.

"I'm so glad to see you, sire," she said brightly. "You came just in time to eat."

Goél smiled, and this made him look much younger. He was deeply tanned, and his teeth were very white against the darkness of his skin. "I always manage to come at suppertime. But first, let me introduce my companion." He turned to the young man who stood beside him. "This is Teanor. Teanor, you have heard of the Seven Sleepers. This is Sarah. And this is Abigail."

Teanor was a slight young man, not a great deal taller than Sarah. He was very trim and fit, though, and his tan was even darker than that of Goél. He had light brown hair, cut short, and his eyes were deep-set and inquisitive. "I have heard of the Seven Sleepers," he murmured.

"Come inside, sire," Sarah said. "It won't take long to grill steaks for you."

The two men entered the little house, and as Sarah scurried about preparing food for their guests, she listened to Goél talk with Abbey, mostly about their last adventure. From time to time she turned to glance at the young man. He said nothing. He appeared worried, and she wondered about his relationship with Goél.

The steaks were cooked very quickly, and the two men ate hungrily. When they had finished, Sarah set out the remains of the chocolate pie, and Abbey served large cups of steaming tea.

Finally Goél leaned back and nodded. "That was as fine a meal as I can remember. You girls are both marvelous cooks."

"It was good indeed," Teanor said. "I thank you."

Goél turned his eyes on Teanor and studied him a moment or two. Then he turned back to Sarah and Abbey. "Where are the boys?"

"Oh, they went out on a hunting trip," Sarah said. "They may not be back for a time."

"I wish they were here," Goél said quietly. Then he said, "Teanor's people are called the Cloud People."

"What a wonderful name! Why are they called that, Teanor?" Sarah asked.

The young man smiled. "We live in high places."

"The Cloud People," Goél said, "were on good terms with their neighbors the Earth Dwellers until recent years. Some time ago, however, things began to change. Since I must go now, perhaps you could tell them about it, Teanor. The Dark Lord is at work, and I am needed in another place. I thank you again."

When the farewells had been said and their leader was gone, the young man Teanor sat up straight in his chair. "What Goél told you is true. As my father has told me, at one time our people and the Earth Dwellers were friendly. But a few years ago their chief, whose name is Maroni, fell under the influence of a high priest called Nomus. He is an evil man and demands human sacrifices for their god, Nimbo."

"Human sacrifices!" Sarah exclaimed. "How terrible!"

"It is evil indeed!" Teanor said. "They trap our young men and make slaves out of them. They trap women and children and sacrifice them to their god."

Sarah liked the young man. He seemed earnest and sincere. "So you came to Goél for help?"

"Yes. Our king, Celevorn, has sent me for help. We need fierce warriors to overcome the Earth Dwellers. And we had heard of Goél's servants the Seven Sleepers."

"It will be an honor to help your people."

Teanor said, "My own brother is a captive of the Earth Dwellers. I must save him. How long before the warriors return?"

"I'm not sure. Perhaps two or three days, but I hope not that long."

"Then, alas, I cannot wait for them. I must return in the morning and do what I can."

Sarah did not argue but showed Teanor a place to sleep in Dave's room.

All night long she tossed and turned. She was concerned with Teanor's plight and also for some reason was still angry with the boys for having left. Still, she knew that this was not their fault. They had no way of knowing this emergency would come.

Finally she drifted off to sleep, but she awoke early, still thinking of what to do.

She woke up Abbey. "Wake up, Abbey!" she said, standing over Abbey's cot and shaking her shoulder.

"What—what is it? What time is it?"

"Abbey, we've got to help Teanor."

"Well, of course we will. We've already agreed on that. Did you wake me up to tell me that?"

"Get up. We've got to talk."

Abbey arose reluctantly, and the two girls dressed. Dawn was beginning to break as they went into the kitchen and began to prepare a quick breakfast. When it was ready, Sarah went to Dave's room and knocked on the door. "Teanor, are you awake?"

"Yes." The door opened. The young man was fully dressed and seemed ready to leave. He even had his knapsack on his back.

"Come and have breakfast before you go."

"I am in a great hurry."

"You have time to eat, and, besides, I have something to tell you."

Teanor hesitated but then nodded. "Very well," he said.

Sarah led the young man to the table, where they set a good breakfast before him, and the three sat down to eat.

When Teanor was finished, he said, "I thank you for the meal, but I must hurry."

"But you came to get help, and you haven't yet received it."

"I know," he said sadly. "But I cannot even sleep for thinking about our poor people."

"Teanor, I have news for you. Abbey and I have decided to accompany you on your return home."

For a moment there was total silence, and then Teanor exclaimed, "What good would that do?"

"But didn't you come to get help?"

"I came to get *warriors!* I cannot put my trust in females!"

Ordinarily such words as these would have caused an argument, but Sarah understood Teanor's position. "You don't understand," she said. "Josh and the others will join us as soon as they return."

"They would never be able to find my home."

"Yes, they would. I've thought it all out carefully. We'll leave them a note and a map. The three of us can go on together, and as soon as they get back, they can follow."

But Teanor shook his head firmly. "That is not why I came. I do not need females. I need men."

This caused Sarah's pride to rise up. "You may be surprised to find out what we can do." She did not want to boast about her own accomplishments, but she felt that she was being challenged.

Teanor studied the two girls, then got up. "I thank you for the food, but I must return."

"Give us half an hour, and we'll be ready," Sarah said quickly.

Teanor hesitated. "All right," he said. "But I will not have time to wait longer for you. And if you cannot keep up, you must return."

The two girls immediately got their backpacks and began to throw their gear together. They put on their best traveling boots and wore their swords at their sides. Sarah, of course, carried her bow and a quiver of excellent arrows. Then she wrote a note for the boys.

Finally, at her urging, Teanor drew a map leading to the home of the Cloud People.

"It is a difficult journey and full of danger. I still am not certain they can find their way."

"They can find us." Sarah nodded confidently. "Now we're ready."

He gave a shrug. "Follow me if you wish," he said. "But I will never put my life in the hands of females."

Sarah smiled. "We'll see if we can't change your mind."

3

Danger in the Forest

Sarah wiped her face, for perspiration was running down her cheeks. Her legs were trembling with weakness, but she tried to let nothing of this show in her expression. Glancing over at Abbey, Sarah saw that she was in even worse condition. The younger girl's face was pale, and she was obviously gasping for breath.

"It's all right, Abbey. We'll have to stop pretty soon. We can't walk all night." The sun was almost hidden now, and darkness was falling.

"I think he could!" Abbey shot a resentful glance at Teanor, who tramped along far ahead of them. He seemed to be absolutely tireless.

Both girls had determined that they would not lag behind, but both groaned with relief when at last he turned and called back, "We shall camp here for the night."

Trying to conceal her gasping for breath, Sarah said, "It looks like a good spot."

Looking around, he said, "We will make the fire in this place. I will get the wood, and you will cook."

As Teanor moved away into the thickening darkness, Abbey snapped, "He's certainly bossy!"

"Yes, he is." Sarah slipped off the backpack and rubbed her shoulders where the straps had cut in. Then she put it down against a tree and began to unpack it, saying, "I don't see why we can't just eat a cold supper tonight. I'm too tired to cook, but don't tell him that."

Teanor was back soon, carrying dry wood, and soon the yellow blaze of the fire he kindled was pushing the shadows back. Once he had made the fire, he sat down and watched the girls prepare the food.

They had brought steaks, and as Sarah cooked them, she said, "This is the last fresh meat we'll have unless we shoot something."

Teanor did not answer. He was staring into the fire and seemed unaware of their presence. He shook himself only when Abbey said, "The meal's ready." Then he reached out and took the tin plate from her and said, "I suppose you can eat with me this time."

"What do you mean eat with you? Where else would we eat?" Sarah asked.

"Females do not eat with men."

"What are you talking about?" Abbey asked. "'Females do not eat with men.' Of course, women eat with men."

"That may be your way, but it is not the way of the Cloud People." The young man bit into his steak at once and ate hungrily. He did not bother to say thank you, a discourtesy that Sarah noticed with disapproval. Finally, when he had finished eating and had slaked his thirst at the small stream that ran close by, he said, "We will leave at dawn. Come."

"Come where?" Sarah asked in bewilderment.

"We must climb the tree, of course."

"Climb the tree!" Abbey exclaimed. "What in the world for?"

"To avoid danger! Don't tell me you're thinking of sleeping here on the earth!"

"But that's what we always do!" Sarah exclaimed.

"You're fools then! What if a lion comes along, or a bear? Or an Earth Dweller? What would you do?"

24

Sarah stared at the young man, then shook her head. "I'm not sleeping in any tree, and that's final!"

"Neither am I," Abbey said. "We have our blankets, and we're going to sleep right by this fire."

"Do as you please," Teanor said. Without another word, he turned and leaped up to catch a lower branch. Sarah was amazed at how quickly he shinnied far up into the tree with all the agility of a monkey.

"Well," she said softly, sitting back down by the fire and reaching for her blanket. "What do you think of Teanor?"

"I don't like him," Abbey said. "He has no thoughtfulness about him at all. He didn't once stop today and ask us if we were all right. He didn't say ten words."

"I guess he's worried—both about his people and about his brother. Sounds like a bad situation." Sarah's muscles ached. She unrolled her blanket and climbed into it.

Abbey did the same, but for a time both girls lay awake.

The fire crackled and slowly settled into a bed of red coals that sent out a warm glow.

"You know," Abbey said sleepily, "I keep thinking maybe we should have waited, Sarah."

"Waited for what?"

"Waited for the boys to come back."

"Oh, we're all right. They can follow later."

Abbey, however, despite her fatigue, seemed concerned. "I'm truly worried about it, Sarah. Somehow I think Goél would expect us to all go together. We always have."

"No. We haven't always. I remember the time you ran off to the World of the Underground without us."

There was silence except for the crackling of the

fire. Then Abbey said, "And I've been thinking about that time. I was too hasty. I got myself into a great deal of trouble because I did that."

"It's different this time."

"I don't think it is. And I wish we had waited for them."

"But just think," Sarah said. "If we could bring peace between these two tribes all by ourselves, that would show the boys something, wouldn't it?"

"I suppose so, but it sounds like peacemaking is going to be quite a job. Good night, Sarah."

Sarah fell asleep almost at once as soon as she said good night.

It seemed that she had barely dropped off, however, when she heard Teanor saying, "Well, I see you're still here. Get up. We must get on the trail."

Sarah sat up abruptly. It was still pitch dark. "Why, it's the middle of the night!" she exclaimed.

"It will be light in an hour. We can cover several miles by that time."

Sarah and Abbey struggled out of their blankets. They groped around in the darkness and repacked their gear. They all ate some trail mix, and soon the girls were stumbling after their guide.

The second day turned out to be worse than the first, although neither Sarah nor Abbey would have admitted it.

Teanor did not look back often. He stopped once at midmorning and again at noon to eat a little trail mix but said little. He seemed troubled and even uncomfortable.

Once Abbey said, "Sarah, I'm starting to think he's just shy with girls."

"No, I don't think so," Sarah said slowly. She had

been thinking about Teanor's behavior. "I think it's that we don't even *count* to him. Didn't you hear what he said about the Cloud People women not eating with the men?"

"I heard him. It doesn't sound like a place I'd like to live."

"Well, we won't have to live there," Sarah said wearily. "Right now I'm just hoping we *get* there."

When they had traveled hard for two days and one morning, Teanor said, "From here on, the way is *very* dangerous." There was a frown on his face, and he fingered the knife at his belt. It was the only weapon he carried, except for a staff.

"Why is it dangerous?" Sarah asked.

"Because this is the land of the Earth Dwellers."

"Why do you call them Earth Dwellers?" Abbey was looking curiously around at the terrain. It seemed rather wild. Trees towered high, and the way through them looked difficult.

"Because they dwell on earth," Teanor said impatiently.

Sarah could not help smiling. "Well, of course. Earth Dwellers would dwell on earth."

"Yes. Why in the world did I ask?" Abbey asked.

"Come. And keep your eyes open."

The forest grew thick, and the briars tore at the girls' clothes. Somehow Teanor was able to slip through the brambles, but both girls suffered rents in their clothing.

From time to time they passed through open places, where the blue sky was clear overhead. At other times they traveled through thick forest in which the trees practically blotted out the sky and the sun.

"I've never seen forest any thicker than this," Sarah

muttered. She stopped to free her ankle from a thorny vine that had wound around it. She winced and said, "The briars are going to tear our clothes to pieces."

Abbey seemed too tired to say much. She devoted all her strength to keeping up with Teanor. "I hope we get to these Cloud People pretty soon," she gasped.

Now they emerged into a small field. Here the sky was clear overhead, and almost in the middle of the field Sarah saw a beautiful flowering shrub growing. "Look at that!" she exclaimed. "That's the most beautiful bush I've seen for a long time!"

"It *is* beautiful," Abbey said. "I'm going to pluck one of those blossoms. I never saw color like that."

Abbey started toward the shrub. The bush was well over seven feet tall. It spread out in all directions, and its blooms were a mix of pink, crimson, and even a lovely bluish shade. Abbey loved flowers, and she probably planned to put one of those blue blossoms in her hair.

But Teanor was yelling. He had been well ahead of them, but now he was running with all his might back toward Abbey, who had almost reached the flowering bush.

Abbey stopped to look at him. "What's wrong?"

Teanor did not answer. He continued running toward her at top speed. His head was down, and his legs churned. When he was about ten feet away, he threw himself at her in a headlong dive.

Sarah screamed, "What's wrong?" But then she saw something that she could not believe. The beautiful plant suddenly let loose what appeared to be a tiny arrow. It flew through the air so quickly that she got only a glimpse of it, but she heard Teanor cry out as it struck him.

"Teanor, what is it?"

"Get out of here!" he yelled. He rolled over, yanked Abbey to her feet, and started running again, pulling her along.

Sarah too, frightened by his behavior, ran as hard as she could. When they got to the line of trees, Teanor stopped. He held out his arm. "It got me! That's an arrow tree. Why did you even get near it?"

"I—I thought the blossoms were beautiful," Abbey said. She was staring at the slender shaft that had struck Teanor's forearm. It was about the length of a pencil, and the tip was still buried in his flesh.

"What is that?" Sarah cried out.

"It's a poison barb. It's got to come out—and quick!" he said.

Sarah swallowed hard. "I'll help you." She reached out to help, and Teanor jerked his arm back.

"No! There's a barb in there. If it stays in, I'll die. But you can't just pull it out."

"Then, how do we get it out?"

"Push it through," he said. His face was pale and perspiration was gathering on his brow. "Quickly! I can already feel the effects of the poison. Push it through and cut off the barb."

Sarah stared at him for only a second longer, but she could see with her own eyes that he was weakening. Quickly she grasped his arm and said, "Abbey, hold his arm still." She waited until Abbey had taken Teanor's wrist, then grasping the shaft, she took a deep breath. *I've got to do this quickly*, she thought. She gave one hard push.

Teanor slumped to the ground. But the barb was out.

Sarah whipped her knife from its sheath, cut off

the barb, then with a swift movement pulled the shaft free.

Teanor's eyes were closed. "I'm going to be very sick," he whispered. "We must get to safety."

"I've got some ointment in my bag," Abbey said. "Let me put it on your arm."

Teanor lay still while the two girls treated the ugly wound and bound it. Then he struggled to his feet. "We've got to get out of here at once. If the Earth Dwellers catch us here, it will be death."

For a short time the girls had to help him walk, but when dark came on again, Teanor looked upward and said, "It's time. We must climb this tree."

Sarah too looked up, and she gasped. "I can't do that!"

"You'll have to."

As sick as Teanor was, he was still able to pull himself up to the first limb. He did not even look back but simply called, "Quickly! There are evil things on this ground after dark. Climb the tree!"

Sarah turned to Abbey. "Look. I can never climb with this backpack, and neither can you."

"We can't leave them here. Some beast might get them."

Sarah had already thought that out. She pulled a strong line from her bag, fastened the two knapsacks together, and then tied the line to them. "Go on up. When we are up, we'll pull it after us."

Abbey swallowed hard and nodded.

It was a difficult climb. Sarah was afraid of heights, and Abbey did not particularly like them. But up they went. Fortunately, the branches were spaced so that they could reach them easily. They went up—up—up—until finally they came to Teanor, who had wedged himself between two strong limbs. His lips were pale, and his eyes were closed.

"We'll have to tie him to the tree. He might roll off and kill himself," Sarah said. She pulled up the bags, and tied them tightly. Then the two girls bound Teanor firmly to a large branch.

"What about us? We might fall, too," Abbey said nervously.

"We're going to tie ourselves in. Find the most comfortable place you can. I'll tie you in. Then I'll tie myself."

The girls crawled carefully among the branches, for it was a great way to the ground. Abbey found a large crotch where she could almost lie down, and Sarah tied her to it, leaving her arms and legs free.

"Now at least you can't fall out," she said.

"What about you?"

"Now I'll do the same for myself."

Five minutes later, Sarah was tied in, and she no sooner was than she realized she was thirsty. *I should have taken a canteen out*, she thought. She also realized that Teanor was moaning. *He's probably thirsty, too.* So she untied herself, climbed over to the backpacks, and took out two canteens. One of them she took to Abbey. "Better keep it with you, Abbey," she said. "It's going to be a long night."

She crawled then to where Teanor was twisting about, seeming to be having a nightmare. She held his head and managed to get some water into him. She always carried with her a NuWorld drug that was somewhat like aspirin. She got one of the pills down his throat and then another. After that she sat with him until he grew quiet.

Sarah crept back to her place. She tied herself in

again and prepared for a miserable night. And it was a miserable night.

Soon darkness came. From time to time, there came howlings and vicious snortings from the ground below. Sarah would doze off, and then terrible cries— a fight between wild animals perhaps—would wake her.

More than once, she found herself thinking, *Abbey was right. We should have waited for the boys.* It was too late, however, to do anything about that. And finally, at some time, she dropped off into a fitful sleep.

4

Land of the Cloud People

The sun was beginning to peep over the horizon when Sarah crept cautiously to where Teanor was beginning to stir. She found that her muscles were sore from remaining in the same position. "Are you feeling better?" she asked anxiously.

"I . . . think so." He blinked and looked at the ropes that held him in the crotch of the tree. Then he smiled faintly and said, "I have never fallen out of a tree in my life."

"I know, but I was afraid you might. You were delirious and tossing around."

"Well, untie me. We've got to get out of here."

Quickly Sarah unfastened the ropes, then saw that Abbey was now loose also. "Are you all right, Abbey?"

"I'm sore as a boil." Abbey groaned. She tried to move her arms and legs and winced. "Sleeping in a tree is not what I like to do the most."

Teanor laughed. "You two just don't know much about trees," he said.

Sarah saw that he was moving carefully and his arm was swollen. Nevertheless, he made it safely to the ground. The girls lowered their knapsacks, then followed.

Teanor looked about worriedly and said, "This is the ancient forest. It's not a good place."

When Sarah glanced around, she saw a twisting trail. "Is that the way we go?" she asked.

"Yes. That trail will lead us to my home."

"Let's have something to eat first. I'm starving," Abbey said.

The other two agreed, and they ate a cold breakfast. Then they started out.

Teanor did not keep as fast a pace as the day before, and Sarah knew that he was not yet over the effects of the poison dart. He did not complain, however. Often he glanced around warily.

"You'd better keep that bow and your swords handy," he said. "There are many strange beasts that roam in these woods."

"I guess we're used to that," Sarah said. "We've seen everything from saber-toothed tigers to snake people in NuWorld."

The sun rose higher, and the way grew even more difficult. Brambles and briars clawed at their clothing, tearing rents in them and scratching their hands as they attempted to pull them away.

Finally they took a break and sat down beside a brook. The girls washed their faces, and both drank from the small, clear stream, but their guide was watching the woods.

"That was good," Sarah said, drying her face with a handkerchief. "I'd like to take a swim. I'm so hot and sweaty and dirty."

Abbey was pulling at her hair. She said, "Yuck! My hair is filthy!"

"If you'd cut it off as our females do," Teanor said, "it wouldn't be so much trouble."

"Cut my hair off!" Abbey was indignant. "I'll not do any such thing."

But Sarah was thinking of more important things than a shampoo for Abbey's hair. "Do you think the boys will be able to follow your map?" she asked Teanor. "This is a twisted sort of trail."

"I don't know," he said wearily. "It would have been far better if they had been back from their hunt and I could have led them. But then *you* insisted on coming."

Sarah knew that the young man was upset with her. As a matter of fact, she was upset with herself, but it was too late now to do anything about what they had done. "They are good woodsmen," she said brightly. "I'm sure they'll find us."

Teanor started to get up. "We'd better get going," he said. "We don't have—" He broke off suddenly, then yelled, "Look out! It's a scorpion!"

"A scorpion?" Sarah had in mind one of the small NuWorld scorpions that she had seen before. They were no more than a few inches across, and she said, "Don't worry. I'm not afraid of scorpions."

At that moment Abbey screamed and scrambled to her feet. "*Sarah!*" she cried and began fumbling for her sword.

Sarah looked up to see one of the most frightening sights she had ever seen. It was a scorpion all right, but it was a monstrous one, the size of a young horse.

"Get out of here!" Teanor cried. He grabbed for his staff to defend them, but Sarah saw that such a fight would be hopeless.

"Run! I'll stop him!" she cried. She seized her bow and quickly notched an arrow. She drew back the string, aware that she would have only one shot, and she was not certain that one arrow would stop this beast.

The scorpion was much like the smaller ones that she had seen, except that it had a spotted body and a snakelike head. It scrambled along on six legs. A seg-

35

mented tail curved over the creature's body, and at the tip of it a long stinger was poised. The poison from such a monster would be tremendous.

Sarah breathed a cry to Goél for his help and drew back the bow. As the terrible creature scuttled toward her with its stinger ready, she loosed the arrow.

It struck the scorpion exactly in the center of its open mouth.

The momentum of the beast carried it forward a few steps until it was only a few feet away from Sarah. She had no time to move. She knew if the creature fell on her, she would be crushed. With a burst of desperation she threw herself to one side, and the scorpion's stinger descended right where she had stood.

"Sarah, are you all right?" Abbey cried.

"Y-yes, I'm all right," Sarah said, and she scrambled to her feet. The beast had fallen to one side, and its beady eyes had already lost their fierce red light.

Teanor walked up and looked silently at the scorpion. He did not speak for a moment, but then he looked at Sarah seemingly with new respect. "So even a girl can fight," he muttered.

But Abbey cried, "That was a wonderful shot, Sarah! If you hadn't gotten him right in the head, he would have killed you."

"I think I had a little help with that one. Thank you, Goél," Sarah said. She found that her hands were shaking, but she concealed that from the other two. "I hope there are no more like this around."

"There are a lot more of them," Teanor said worriedly. "And the quicker we get out of here the better. Now let us go."

He led the way again, along a path that twisted like a snake. The attack of the scorpion had driven away all thoughts of rest, and they traveled as hard as they could.

At noon they stopped for a brief break. With her bow, Sarah had brought down a tiny deerlike creature, which they quickly dressed and cooked over a small fire. The meat seemed to put new life into them all.

Unexpectedly, Teanor suddenly said, "You are a wonderful shot with that bow. None of our people have bows."

"How do you fight your enemies, then?"

"We really don't. We have no enemies except the Earth Dwellers. And they can't get at us."

Sarah considered that. Then she sat looking up at the trees that towered overhead. "These are the biggest trees I've ever seen," she said.

He looked at her with surprise in his eyes. "These! Why, these are just saplings!"

"Saplings?" Abbey cried. "What are you talking about?"

"These are not big trees," he protested. "Truly, don't you have trees this big in your world?"

"Back in OldWorld, the biggest trees were the sequoias, and these are much bigger than they were."

Teanor just shook his head. "I would not want to live in a world that had spindly little trees like this."

The two girls looked at each other.

Sarah said, "Then I'm anxious to see your big trees, if these are small ones."

They began their journey again and traveled hard. They stopped only once more, about midafternoon, and Sarah looked about her, surprised. The trees here indeed were bigger! They rose to the sky like towers.

Teanor saw her looking up. "Well," he said with satisfaction. "Now you're seeing something like a tree."

"How much farther is your home?" Abbey asked. "I'm exhausted."

"It's not far. We'll be there in an hour if we move fast."

As they trekked through the vast forest, Sarah was more and more astonished. The trees rose hundreds of feet over their heads. And there were no branches for at least fifty feet in the air. She once stopped long enough to touch one and found that the bark was not rough and scaly but smooth and almost moist.

"It would be hard to climb one of these," she murmured, looking upward.

Teanor laughed. "Difficult indeed! And we are safe now, unless we run into a band of wandering Earth Dwellers."

"Do they live close to here?"

"It's quite a distance to their village, but they come here to hunt the deer and other animals for food. That's how my people get captured."

The ground was level now and covered with fine mosslike grass. Sunshine filtered through the foliage far overhead, and there was a constant murmuring as the wind rustled through the leaves.

At last Teanor stopped. He took a deep breath, then turned to the girls and smiled. "Well," he said. "This is my home."

Sarah looked about them and saw nothing but the trunks of the enormous trees. "Where is the village?" she asked.

Teanor laughed again, then pointed upward. "There," he said.

Both girls gazed up into the tree. Sarah could see nothing except foliage. Far above them, the first branches grew straight out. The branches were as large as the trunks of the OldWorld trees she was accustomed to seeing. They spread wide, making a kind of canopy, so that she could not see the branches above.

"Up there?" Sarah asked.

"Yes."

"You live in a village in the *trees?*" Abbey gasped.

"That's why they call us the Cloud People. Sometimes, when the weather is right, the clouds cover the tops of the trees, and we actually live in the clouds. Sometimes above them."

"But how do you get up there?" Sarah asked.

"Like this." He put two fingers in his mouth and gave a shrill whistle that hurt her ears. It was some sort of a signal, for suddenly a stout looking vine descended from somewhere in the foliage above.

"This is the way we get up," he said. He scrambled up the vine as agile as any monkey Sarah had ever seen. But he stopped twenty feet up and smiled down at them. "Well, come on. Are you going to stay there all day?"

"But—but we can't climb a vine like that!" Sarah said.

"No. I didn't think you could." Hanging on easily by one hand, he whistled again and then slid back down to the ground. "For old people and babies we have to make other arrangements. And for girls too, it seems. Although our own females can climb the vines almost as well as men."

The two girls kept looking upward, and Sarah saw something descending. It came down in fits and jerks, and when it finally came completely into her vision, she exclaimed, "Why, it's a basket!"

There were two of them, each about the size of a large barrel back in OldWorld. Vines were attached to them, and they landed on the ground with a thump.

"There you are, Sarah. This one's for you," Teanor said. "And you get into that one, Abbey."

"You mean they're going to pull us up?"

"There's no other way to get there, and you can't stay here!"

At once Abbey, who had little fear of heights, jumped into her basket. "Get in, Sarah. It's just like an elevator."

Sarah swallowed hard and said, "All right. I suppose I'll have to."

"You're afraid of going up high?" Teanor asked with astonishment. "I never knew anybody who was afraid of heights."

"I'm not afraid. I'm just careful," Sarah said defiantly. Slowly she put herself into the basket and held onto the edge of it until her knuckles turned white. "All right," she whispered. "I guess I'm ready."

Teanor whistled another signal, somewhat different from the others, and Sarah gave a short cry as her basket suddenly lurched. Then it started rising, and she closed her eyes.

Abbey, however, seemed delighted. "Look, Sarah!" she cried. "You're missing it all!"

Sarah cautiously opened her eyes and looked. The ground seemed to be very far below them. Her basket kept rising steadily, although rather jerkily. She watched the ground slowly fall away from her. But she hung on and glanced upward.

Teanor was climbing a vine above them, as easily as he had moved along the ground. The muscles in his back and arms were well developed. He smiled down at her and then waited until her basket reached his level. "So how do you like it, Sarah?"

"It's—it's fine," she managed to say. She did not

want to show fear, and she forced herself to look down again. It was indeed a beautiful sight, with the majestic trees rising everywhere and the green ground underneath.

"Look above you, Sarah!" Abbey suddenly yelled.

Sarah turned her head upward and saw what seemed to be a platform built on a huge limb extending outward from the trunk. There were large square openings here and there in it, and she saw that the vine that pulled her basket disappeared into one of them. Not knowing what to expect, she held onto the side of the basket as it passed through one opening at the same time Abbey's basket was drawn up through another.

A small group of people was gathered on the platform, and two men seized Sarah's basket and set it down with a thump.

Teanor appeared suddenly. He gave himself a flip off his vine and landed on the very edge. Sarah gasped. She knew it was hundreds of feet to the ground, but he seemed to have no fear at all.

Teanor, however, saw the alarm in her eyes. "It's all right, Sarah," he said. "You're in my home now. Welcome to the land of the Cloud People!"

5

A Strange City

Sarah and Abbey stood on the tree platform. It was made of small saplings fastened together with vines. For a moment Sarah became almost ill, for, in spite of the size of the trees, she could feel the platform swaying under her. A brisk breeze rustled through the glossy green leaves that formed the canopy overhead. Looking up, she could see blue sky. Indeed, the clouds seemed very close, white and fleecy.

Both Sarah and Abbey glanced down at the vines that had pulled them up. They ran through a wheel and an overhead branch, and the system had worked like a pulley.

Like Teanor, the men who had pulled them up were small and wiry but with highly developed shoulder and arm muscles. They all wore simple garments of rough woven cloth and had a golden tan.

"First, I want to show you our city," Teanor said proudly. "This way," He turned and went straight to the edge of the platform.

Sarah began following him but then stopped, for she saw that a swinging bridge led to another, larger platform where something like a house was built.

The structure seemed very fragile. It was made of bamboo stalks tied together with vines. The only support was a thick vine rope on each side. The bridge dipped down in the center and swayed back and forth in the breeze.

Teanor stepped onto it.

"I can never cross on that," Sarah gasped.

"It's all right," he said. "I'll help you." He came back and took her by the hand. "Now you hold onto the rope on the other side, and I'll hold you on this side."

Sarah wished she were anywhere in the world but in the land of the Cloud People. But she had learned to face danger in many forms, and now she took a deep breath and gritted her teeth. "All right. But don't let go of me."

Teanor led her to the swinging bridge, and his hand was tight on hers. "Don't be nervous," he said. "You won't fall."

Sarah grasped the rope and stepped out onto the bridge. It swayed under her, and she took short steps. She was afraid to look down. Instead, she kept her eyes on the bamboo house that was built on the far side.

Then she heard Abbey saying from behind her, "It's all right, Sarah. This is fun!"

That gave Sarah new determination, and she started to move across the swinging bridge more quickly.

"That's the way. You see. There's nothing to it." Teanor smiled.

They reached the other side, and as soon as she planted her feet on the platform, Sarah felt better. The whole platform was swaying, but it was not as precarious as the bridge itself. She looked back to see Abbey walking across as easily as if it were a cement sidewalk.

Abbey leaped onto the platform and cried, "This is wonderful, Teanor!"

"I'm glad you like it. Now, this is not my house, but all houses are about the same here. These are visitors to Cloud Land—Sarah and Abbey," he said to the man who stood at the door, watching with amazement. "Do you mind if we show her your house?"

"No, not at all. Come inside."

Sarah and Abbey stepped in. It was much like a tree house, Sarah thought. The floor was of saplings covered with a rough brown mat made of vines. The furniture, what there was of it, all seemed lightweight. There were windows on every side, and she wondered what it was like when it rained. *Very wet, I would suppose.*

Over to one side was a small fireplace where the cooking was done, and a woman with long hair stood there, shyly watching them.

It did not take long to look at the house. Teanor thanked the man, and they went out.

"His name is Guntor," he said. "He's a very good fisherman."

"What was his wife's name?"

"Oh, the female? I don't recall."

Something about all this troubled Sarah. Guntor himself seemed to make nothing of the woman. *It looks as if he could at least introduce her,* Sarah thought with displeasure. She glanced at Teanor and started to speak, but by that time they were already about to cross another bridge.

She now saw that bridges connected different platforms built on the wide spreading branches. While she was crossing the swaying bridges, which seemed as fragile as spider webs, she did not think of anything except holding on. The ground lay far beneath, and she resolutely did not look down.

However, each time they reached a different platform, she would look at her surroundings. As far as she could see, there were houses and other buildings at the tops of the mighty trees. People were moving around easily from one tree to another. Sometimes people swung on vines that connected various structures. They seemed to be as unconcerned about their safety as if they were walking down a solid road on earth below. There was an airiness and an ease about all their movements that amazed Sarah.

"They're like trapeze artists," she said with amazement.

"What is a trapeze artist?" Teanor asked.

"Well, it's hard to explain. They–they are people that swing and catch each other for the entertainment of others."

"Entertainment!" Teanor frowned. "All we want is to get from one place to another."

Abbey was as wide-eyed as Sarah. "Just look, Sarah," she said. "Even the smallest of them have no fear at all." She pointed to several little children, some of them barely walking, who were playing right on the edge of one of the platforms. They seemed to have no concept of height at all. Abbey shook her head. "I've never seen a place like this."

Another thing that Sarah noticed was that almost every house had plants growing around it. She stopped once to look and saw that a tomato plant was growing out of a clay pot filled with dirt. "That's very clever to do up here," she said to Teanor.

"Oh, we have some very good gardeners among our people. We bring up only the best soil, and there's always plenty of rain and sunshine. So we can grow all the vegetables we need."

The cloud city seemed to spread out over a considerable distance, farther than a village on earth.

Some trees held as many as a half dozen small houses, but often there were only one or two.

Finally Teanor pointed ahead. "And that is the palace. We will find King Celevorn there."

He helped Sarah cross the last bridge, which connected to an enormous platform, much larger than any of the others. Once she was on the solid platform, she was startled to see that the "palace" was constructed on several levels. It was of bamboo, as were all the others, but this building was much more ornate. There were windows on every level, and flowers grew everywhere out of small containers. Servants hurried about, all women as far as Sarah could tell, all plainly dressed, and all eyeing them with apprehension.

"They've never seen anybody like you." Teanor grinned. "Now follow me. The king will be anxious to see you."

Teanor led Sarah and Abbey up several flights of steps. Sarah thought she could still feel the tree moving slightly in the breeze. But that may have been only her imagination, for this was the most enormous tree that she had seen yet. Where they were now must be the trunk, she guessed. It must have been at least twenty feet thick at the top and no telling how large at the bottom.

As they came to a large set of doors covered with a curtain, Teanor spoke to the guard who stood outside with a staff in his hand and a sword in his belt.

"So you found them, eh, Teanor?" He peered at the girls and asked, "Where are the warriors?"

Teanor registered some disgust. "They're on their way—we hope. Is the king receiving?"

"Yes. He got word that you were coming from our sentinels. Go right on in."

The girls entered and found themselves in a spacious room. Several women servants were moving about, and it was obvious that the king had just enjoyed a meal. He was sitting at a table covered with dishes and cups and several wooden platters of food were still before him.

"O King Celevorn, I have found the Seven Sleepers," Teanor announced, and he bowed deeply.

King Celevorn had a goblet in his hand. He set it down, then took a look at the two girls. "Seven Sleepers! I see only two females."

"Yes, sire. The males were gone. But they will come as quickly as they can. This is Sarah, and this is Abigail."

King Celevorn was small, as were all of the Cloud People Sarah had seen. His auburn beard was streaked with gray. He was still strong looking, however, and his eyes were clear as he studied them. Then he turned to a young man sitting on his right and said, "I am disappointed. I expected more."

"This is Jere, son of King Celevorn," Teanor explained quickly.

Jere was a handsome youth, lean and strong as was his father. His hair was rich with glints of fiery red in it, and he grinned in a friendly way as he stared at the new arrivals. "I see I will have to write a poem about this."

"A poem!" King Celevorn snorted. "That's what we need—more poetry!" He looked angrily at his son. "If you would stop writing poetry and singing songs, we might get some defense against the Earth Dwellers."

"Well, Father, battles come and go, but a poem lasts forever."

Sarah was rather shocked at the son's attitude. He

seemed totally unconcerned with the people's problems, and his face was unlined with worries of any kind.

King Celevorn frowned in apparent disgust, then rose and approached the girls. He was very little taller than Sarah, but his eyes were sharp and penetrating as he looked at her. He looked then at Abigail and finally threw up his hands. "Two females, Teanor! I send you out to get warriors, and this is what you come back with!"

At once Sarah began to explain. "Sire, I ask your pardon. It was my fault that the boys were gone, but we left a map, and they will be here soon."

King Celevorn listened politely, but disappointment was etched across his face and in his eyes. Finally he held up both hands in a gesture of helplessness. "Well, we must wait, I suppose. Find the females a place to stay, Teanor."

"Yes, do," Jere said quickly. "And then I'll be glad to hear the adventures of the Seven Sleepers." He got to his feet and came over to Abbey, smiling at her. "I will write an ode to the fair Sleepers, for, indeed, I had not expected such beauty."

Sarah was aware that a good-looking boy was never a matter of indifference to Abbey. She was probably wishing her hair was arranged better and that she'd had time to put on her makeup.

But Abbey smiled back at the prince. "I will be happy to tell you what I know, Prince Jere," she assured him.

"Both of you, come with me," Teanor said. "I'll find you a place to stay."

After they had crossed the bridge leading away from the palace, Sarah said, "The prince and his father —they don't seem to get along too well."

"No, they don't. And the king is right. Prince Jere cares for nothing but play."

"But what's wrong with play?" Abbey demanded.

"It doesn't help us with our problem. All these songs and poems he writes. What good are they against the weapons of the Earth Dwellers? They haven't gotten my brother released."

Sarah said nothing. She knew that politics were always rather difficult.

The girls followed Teanor across several bridges until finally they came to a moderate-sized house.

"You will stay here," he said. "I will bring you a female who will help you get settled in." With that, Teanor abruptly plunged out into space.

Both Sarah and Abbey let out screams.

But he caught a vine that was anchored above and swung quickly to another platform.

"Well, *I'll* never go from one house to another that way," Abbey breathed. "I thought he was going to kill himself."

Sarah would not even go to the edge of the platform and look down. It made her dizzy. "Let's go inside," she said.

They found that the place was a house much like the one they had seen earlier. It was one room with a table and chairs. Pegs were driven into the walls for garments. There was a small cabinet, and a place for a cooking fire had been created out of rocks and mortar. The smoke simply rose up and went through a hole in the roof. There were several pots and pans made out of clay.

"Pretty primitive living, Abbey," Sarah said.

"Very primitive. I wonder how you take a bath around here."

It did not take long to explore their new home, and both were getting restless by the time a woman entered. She was young and petite with blonde hair and blue eyes.

Teanor entered behind her. "This is Enid. She will see that you have food. Enid, take care of them."

"Yes. I will," the girl said. She bowed almost slavishly to Teanor, who paid her no attention at all. Sarah quickly noted the way the girl's eyes followed the youth as he left them.

"I'm Sarah, and this is Abbey, Enid," she said as soon as Teanor was gone.

Enid bowed. "I will help you with anything I can." Her eyes were still creeping around to the door.

"You like the young man, don't you?" Sarah asked with a smile.

Enid flushed but shook her head. "No. What can I bring you?"

"Well, I'd like a bath," Abbey said. "Is there any way we could do that? We both brought soap and a change of fresh clothing."

"Oh yes. Come this way. My own home is this one next door."

The two girls followed Enid, and as they moved along the platforms, crossing two more bridges, Sarah questioned her. "Are your parents here, Enid?"

"They are. My mother is Ione. My father is Celevorn."

Sarah was shocked. "You're the daughter of the *king?*"

"Oh yes."

"But that makes you a princess!" Abbey said.

"No. I'm merely a servant."

Sarah could not understand this, and she shot a

questioning glance at Abbey, who also appeared shocked. "Then you are the sister of Prince Jere."

"He is my half brother. We do not have the same mothers."

"But I don't understand," Abbey said. "Why don't you live in the palace?"

Enid gave her a questioning look. "Females do not live in the palace. Only men."

"What about the women?"

"We live elsewhere. We serve the men," Enid said quietly.

Something is wrong about this, Sarah thought. She said nothing more at the time, but she determined to look into the matter later.

The bathhouse proved to be quite simple. It was clever, actually. Rainwater was caught in large containers mounted at the tops of the trees. The water ran down hollow joints of bamboo into a large tank overhead.

"If you get under that, you can release the water by pulling that vine," Enid told them. Then she waited while they lathered and washed their hair. "That smells so good," she said. "What is it?"

"This?" Sarah said with surprise. "Soap." She handed the bar out to Enid, who sniffed it eagerly.

"It smells so good," she repeated.

"We have some extra, if you'd like some, Enid," Sarah said in a kindly fashion.

"Oh, I would! I'd love it!"

They dried off as best they could with the rough cloths that Enid had furnished. They were not thick towels, but they had to serve.

The sun was shining, so they dried their hair while sitting on the bathhouse platform and talking to Enid.

"Enid, do women hold any position of importance here in Cloud Land?"

"Women? Oh no! The men are the important ones. We females only serve them."

Abbey gaped at her and started to speak, but Sarah, knowing Abbey's rather abrupt ways, said quickly, "Back where we lived, women were considered as important as men in most places."

Now Enid gaped at the two girls. "I cannot believe it. Females are not on the same level as men."

"Whoever told you that?" Abbey snapped. She forgot about drying her long blonde hair for the moment. "Of course they're as good as men!"

Enid looked distressed. "Please do not talk like that! No good can come of it."

Sarah tried to understand the social structure in Cloud Land. It appeared to her that men had all the rights and privileges, and women had none. They were little more than slaves in the Cloud People's culture.

When Enid excused herself for a moment, Sarah said, "This is awful, isn't it?"

"Yes. I never heard of such a thing."

"I think it was common in certain places back in OldWorld. In some Eastern countries there were harems, and in parts of Africa the women weren't respected. . . ."

"But that was something we read about in a book," Abbey said sharply. "This is the real thing! The women here have nothing. We've got to do something about this!"

"Now, hold on, Abbey!" Sarah said. "We can't jump in here and change people's customs in twenty-four hours. Besides, the big problem of the moment, apparently, is the Earth Dwellers."

Abbey did not argue. But there was a stubborn set to her lips, and Sarah purposed to watch her.

When they saw Enid coming to take them back to their house, Abbey said wistfully, "I wish we'd waited for the guys, Sarah."

Sarah Collingwood knew in her heart that she had been wrong to act so impulsively. But somehow it was hard for her to admit this. She just said, "Well, they'll get here soon. Come on. Let's go see what there is to eat in Cloud Land."

6
Sarah Decides

The meal that Enid brought Sarah and Abbey was not bad, although neither of them had enough. Each serving consisted of a small helping of something like carrots, one tomato, and a little fish that Enid cooked over a tiny fire. A small bundle of dry sticks furnished the fuel.

There was only a meager amount of firewood left, Sarah noted, and Enid said, "Sometimes it's difficult to get dry wood. We could break off branches, but they would be green and not burn."

"There ought to be plenty of dead wood on the ground," Sarah suggested. "These trees are bound to shed dead branches."

"Oh yes. But the men have to go down and gather them. And that is dangerous."

Sarah ate her fish. It had a very strong flavor, but she was hungry, so said nothing. She only wished that she had some tartar sauce for it.

"Do you ever go down on the ground, Enid?" Abbey asked.

The young woman seemed shocked by the question. "Hardly ever. I've been down only five or six times in my whole life."

"Is that because of the Earth Dwellers?"

"That and the wild beasts." Enid nodded thoughtfully. "We have lost many of our young people to the Earth Dwellers. They become slaves—or else they are sacrificed."

Sarah remembered what Teanor had told them. "What happens to them?" she asked, wanting to know more. "Sacrificed to what?"

"You do not know about Nimbo, the god of the Earth Dwellers?"

"We don't know much," Sarah answered.

"He is a terrible god. And their chief listens to Nomus, the high priest. When things do not go well in the tribe, he tells them they must sacrifice a person. They do not want to sacrifice their own people, so they capture others for this. My own best friend was sacrificed to Nimbo," she said sadly. "I have never gotten over it."

"That's awful!" Abbey exclaimed. "It's probably why your father sent for the Sleepers."

Enid's face brightened with hope. "Yes! Everyone is expecting you to help us. Do you think you can?"

"Well, we have been of some help to others in time past," Sarah said modestly. "It sounds like this Nomus is where the problem lies."

As the girls finished their meal, Abbey asked curiously, "How do you get fish if you don't go down to the ground?"

"I will show you."

They followed Enid across a series of platforms and finally came to one that had no structure on it at all. The platform was very small, no more than ten feet square.

"Now I will show you," she repeated.

Enid picked up a small line and with a hook on one end. From a bucket she took a piece of raw meat and baited the hook. A little stone was tied above the hook, likely to give some stability. "This is what we do," she said. She knelt at the side of the platform.

Sarah sat down abruptly, not daring to stand long on such a precarious perch. Then she and Abbey edged forward and watched as Enid lowered the line. Far beneath was a small stream. They watched the girl maneuver the line until it disappeared into the waters. Enid held the line out to Sarah. "Would you like to try your luck?"

Sarah took the line and held onto it awkwardly. She had always enjoyed fishing but had never experienced anything like this.

"Sometimes we have good luck and catch a big fish. But usually they are very small," Enid admitted.

Before long there was a tug on the line, though, and Sarah yelled, "I got one!" She jerked the line abruptly and felt the weight of the fish. It was evidently fairly large. She began pulling it in, hand over hand.

Abbey was cautiously peering over the side. "You've got one all right, Sarah! Pull him up!"

Sarah's heart was thumping as it always did when she caught a fish. Finally she brought her catch up to where Enid could reach down, grab him by the jaw, and flip him over. "Oh, this is a nice one!" she cried. "He will feed a lot of us!"

Enid struck the fish sharply over the head with a stick, and he lay still. Then she took a knife out of a small box built on the side of the platform and expertly dressed the fish out. She set aside part of it—for bait, she said—then held up the large fillets. "We will divide this among some who need it."

"Is that the way you usually do? Divide things?" Abbey asked curiously.

"Oh yes. There are many poor widows here who are unable to take care of themselves. And small children too. I will show you what we do."

The next half hour was an eye-opener to both girls. Enid went from house to house, at each one cutting off a small portion of the fish. Some of the women they visited were quite old, and other houses had small children. But everywhere they went, the women seemed grateful. They would express their thanks to Sarah as soon as Enid told them that she had caught the fish.

Sarah was made thoughtful by all this. When they went back to their house, carrying very small pieces of the fish for their own supper, Sarah said, "That was very kind of you, Enid."

"No, we just take care of each other here. All of the women do." She looked worried for a moment and said with a frown, "And I didn't think—we should have taken half of the fish to the king."

"No," Abbey said suddenly. "He's got plenty of servants to catch fish for him. Those women don't have anybody. Doesn't he ever feed them?"

"My father actually is a very kind man. But he has many things on his mind."

It was an admission that King Celevorn did sometimes fail to take care of his less able subjects. Sarah noted that and determined that somehow things would have to be different. "Tell me more about your father," she said.

"The king is a good man. He has had only seven wives in his whole life."

"Seven wives!" Abbey exclaimed.

"Uh . . . what happened to the women?"

"My mother is the only one left alive. Her name is Ione. She is the first woman of the king now."

After Sarah listened to Enid explain the system, she said, "It's like *Anna and the King of Siam*."

58

"Who is that?" Enid asked.

"It's a story about a king who had many wives all at one time, and they were all frightened of him. And a woman went to the king's court and convinced him that women were truly important and should not be treated that way."

"My father, the king, would never believe that!"

"You never can tell until you try, Enid," Sarah said firmly.

They spent the rest of the afternoon with the young woman. It was getting late when they heard a strange cry. It was a wailing sound, full of distress and heartbreak.

"What's that, Enid?" Abbey gasped, her face paling.

"It is not good news. I fear another one of our people has been taken."

Enid led them to where a crowd was gathered. There a woman sat with her hair thrown in front of her face. She was rocking back and forth and great sobs shook her body.

"What is it?" Enid said, going over to her.

"They have taken my Romi."

"Romi is taken by the Earth Dwellers?" Enid cried with a gasp.

"He went down to look for food, and they took him. I saw it myself. They took him away. He will be a slave forever—or else he will be sacrificed to Nimbo."

At once Sarah said, "Is it a child? We will go down and take him back."

"You cannot do that."

Sarah turned to see Teanor standing behind them, his face stern. "The Earth Dwellers are already gone. You would never find them, and even if you did, you would be captured, too."

"We can try!" Sarah cried. "You can't just let one of your people be kidnapped without doing anything!"

"That is why I came to you for warriors!" Teanor snapped. "But I got only weak females!" He turned and stalked off, his back straight with anger.

For a time Sarah watched Enid try to comfort the mother. But finally she and Abbey went back to their guesthouse. It was getting dark, so they quickly rekindled the small fire, being very careful to use as little wood as possible. They managed to fry the remaining bits of fish, and they ate another tomato apiece.

"What I wouldn't give for a big fat hamburger as big as a washtub." Abbey sighed. They had eaten everything and knew there would be nothing else until the next day.

Sarah's own stomach was far from filled. She said, "It must be awful to live like this. These are small people and very strong, but they don't get much to eat. Not a balanced diet, I'm sure."

"Sarah, let's go down tomorrow, and we'll kill a deer or something. I'm not as good a shot as you are, but we ought to be able to do something like that."

There were no candles, and the girls could not afford to burn firewood. Their only illumination was the silvery moonlight that came through the open windows. So there was nothing to do after dark but go to bed. They had just a thin covering, and the air was very cool, so both decided to sleep in their clothes in order to keep warm.

Sarah was exhausted. Still, all that they had seen kept her awake. After a while she broke the silence and said, "Are you awake, Abbey?"

"Yes. Can't sleep."

"Neither can I. This is an awful place!"

"It's worse in some ways than places filled with monsters. I feel so sorry for the women and the children here."

"The boys have it pretty easy." Sarah's voice was tinged with bitterness. "It's not a whole lot different from where we just came from."

"Oh, Sarah! Don't be silly. Of course it's different. Are you still mad at Josh?"

Actually Sarah was ashamed of herself. She knew that she had been unjust to Josh and the other boys, but she stubbornly refused to admit it. She changed the subject abruptly. "Did you notice how Enid looks at Teanor?"

"Oh yes. I saw that right away. She's crazy about him."

"And he doesn't know she's alive!" Sarah snapped. "I'd like to pull his hair out." Now she was cross again.

A breeze kept blowing, making a moaning in the tops of the trees. Finally she did drift off, but she slept restlessly.

Sarah heard a footstep, and then a voice said, "Are you awake?"

She sat up at once, reaching for the knife that she always kept handy. She was groggy with sleep, but she said, "Yes. I'm awake." Then she realized that was Enid, waiting for permission to enter. "Come on in, Enid."

"I have brought your breakfast," the young woman said shyly. She held in her hand a small wooden bowl filled with fruit. "These are very good melons. I grew them myself."

By this time, Abbey was awake. The two girls washed their faces, using a small basin, then brushed their hair, tied it back, and sat down to breakfast.

Enid had brought them a small melon each and a bunch of grapes. It was not much, but the melons were indeed delicious.

"These are so good," Abbey said. "And you grew them yourself?"

"Everyone likes my melons. I can never grow enough of them. Most of them go to my father, of course—for his table."

Sarah almost spoke out about that, but she didn't. Instead she said, "This is certainly the best melon I've ever eaten in NuWorld. It must be a lot of work to grow anything up here."

"It is. We have to haul up fresh soil, and we have to be sure the platforms are not rotten. Last year six of our people died from falling through bad platforms. But only five of them were women."

"Only five! Well, that's wonderful!" Abbey muttered. She took a bite of juicy melon and wiped her chin as the juice ran down. "I wish you'd stop putting women down, Enid."

Enid did not understand this at all.

"She means don't say, 'Only women!'" Sarah urged. "One of the things we'll have to teach you is that women and girls are just as important as men and boys."

Enid looked around as if she were afraid someone would hear such talk. "Please! You must not talk like that. If anyone heard it, it would cause trouble."

"I don't care," Sarah said. "Look at you. You're a beautiful girl, and you're in love with Teanor, aren't you?"

"In love? What does that mean?"

Both girls looked at her with shock. Then, "You don't know what it means to be in love?" Abbey exclaimed.

"What does it mean?"

Both Sarah and Abbey tried to explain what courtship was. But it was a hopeless situation. Enid seemingly could not grasp it.

Finally she asked with a puzzled look on her face, "So in your world a young man will come with gifts and sing songs just in order to get a female to be his?"

"Yes," Sarah said firmly. "And that's the way it could be here."

"No. That will never be! All a man has to do if he wants a female, is simply to tell the king. And the king, if he likes the man, will give her to him."

"You're not a piece of fish to be given away!" Abbey cried. "Don't you see that, Enid?"

The two girls struggled on but seemed to make little headway. Finally Abbey threw up her hands. "This is going to be harder than I thought."

"Yes, it is," Sarah agreed.

Enid kept looking at the two girls with wonder. "It must be very different from where you come from. I can't even imagine such a place. And Teanor would never think of me as an equal. All he would do is allow me to serve him."

Well, we're going to change that, Sarah thought but did not speak it.

All that morning, the girls wandered about Cloud Land. They were amazed at the way the Cloud People had adjusted to such a strange environment. They grew their own vegetables, and they also raised a small number of birds kept in cages. They were like pigeons, only larger. These they used for food. They also had small herds of goats, which they used for milk and which they slaughtered from time to time for fresh meat.

They both noticed that none of the men did any work at all. The women cared for the vegetables, killed the birds, did the cooking, and washed the clothes.

"Maybe we'll free some slaves while we're here," Sarah said with determination. "We're going to try."

It was later in the day when Teanor came along. "The king will receive you." He looked over toward Enid, who nodded her head and curtsied to him. "Hello, Enid," he said. "Our clothes need washing."

"Yes, Teanor. I will see to it."

"Did you ever think of washing your own clothes, Teanor?" Abbey asked, staring at him.

"Men don't wash clothes. Women do that," Teanor said. "Come along."

Sarah was seething inside but knew that this was not the time to argue.

Teanor ushered the girls to the palace, and soon they were standing before the king and Prince Jere.

"The men have not come," the king said accusingly.

"It's a hard journey, sire," Sarah said quickly. "And the way is new to them. But I have decided that we will not wait for them."

At that, King Celevorn gave her a puzzled look. "What will you do?" Sarah had formulated a plan the previous night as she lay tossing on her mat. She had thought it over this morning and decided that something had to be done at once. There was no way to know when the boys would come back from their hunting trip, and there was no way to know how long it would take them to follow the twisted path that led to the city in the clouds.

"I have decided to go to the Earth Dwellers myself."

The prince gasped, and then he shook his head.

"You can't do that, Sarah. They will make a slave out of you!"

"Or else sacrifice you to Nimbo," the king said sternly. "Whatever possessed you to think of such a crazy thing? Just like a woman!"

Sarah felt her face flush. She wanted to spit out something in anger but managed to control herself. "I'm going to talk to Chief Maroni. We don't know that he won't listen to reason."

"Reason? That man knows nothing of reason!" Celevorn exclaimed. "The way I understand it, he is totally under the power of Nomus, the high priest."

"He used to be a good man from all we hear," Prince Jere admitted. "But that priest has put a spell on him."

"In any case, it would be suicide for you to go," the king snapped.

Sarah drew herself up to her full height. "I am the servant of Goél. He has sent us into dark and dangerous situations before, and he has never failed us."

"Goél is not here!" the king exclaimed.

"But I am here, and I am his servant! I will leave at once. If you would make me a map so that I may find the village of the Earth Dwellers, I would appreciate it."

King Celevorn eyed Sarah as if she had lost her mind. "You will not need a map," he said bitterly.

"Why not?"

"Because you will be caught by their sentinels. Don't you understand, girl? We rarely dare go down from the trees anymore for fear of being caught. They cannot climb the trees, and that is all that saves us. But once one of our people falls into their hands, they are dead to us."

Sarah Collingwood's courage sometimes faltered, but it did not now. She lifted her chin and said, "King Celevorn, I will show you that a female has courage. I will leave at once, and we will see what a girl can do."

Jere grinned broadly. "I shall write a song about that."

Sarah knew a sudden moment of panic, but she carefully concealed it. "I will leave at once," she repeated. "As soon as I have checked my weapons."

After the two girls were gone, the king muttered, "It will be the Six Sleepers from now on."

"You think the other one will not go with her?"

"She didn't say anything about that, so I doubt it. Well, we can do nothing but wait for the warriors to arrive. After all, she's only a girl."

7
The Trail

Sarah—Abbey? Where are you?"

Josh entered the house eagerly, calling for the two girls as he came. The boys' trip had taken longer than he had thought it would. Still, it had taken him almost four days just to get over his irritation with Sarah. He had not slept well, either, because his problem with her was troubling him.

On the way back, he'd even said to Wash, rather shamefacedly, "I haven't been very wise about this trip, Wash. We should never have left the girls alone."

Wash nodded. "I agree to that," he said. "Besides, I hate to see you quarreling with Sarah. You two are the oldest friends of any of us."

So as Josh burst into the house, he was firmly determined to apologize, something always hard for him. But only silence greeted his calls.

The others filed in, and Reb said, "They're not here? I wonder where they can be."

"Out hunting, probably," Dave said. "Or maybe washing their hair down at the brook."

Jake, however, saw a piece of paper tacked to the wall. "It looks like they left us a note," he said. "See what it says, Josh."

Josh crossed the room and plucked the paper from the wall. He did not read it at once, though, for he was looking at a second paper that was tacked under it. "Why, it's a map," he said.

"A map of what?" Dave asked.

"Don't know," Josh said. "Let me read the note."
He read it aloud:

After you all left, Goél and a young man called
Teanor arrived. Teanor is from the Cloud People.
They are having terrible problems, and Goél wants
us to go help. You are not here, and Teanor was
determined to go back. We are going to accompany him, and we are leaving you a map. Come as
quickly as you can.

Sarah

"Well, ain't that a pretty come-off!" Reb groaned.
"Those girls off on some kind of adventure to some-
place we never heard of—and without us."

Josh's conscience struck him hard then. "We
should have been here," he muttered grimly. "It's all my
fault."

"Where *is* that place that they've gone to?" Dave
asked.

"The Cloud People. Let's see if we can make any
sense out of this map."

He lay the other paper flat on a table, and the boys
all gathered around it. They studied the map, trying to
understand it, and finally Reb exclaimed, "That trail's
as crooked as a snake!"

"It sure is." Wash had a worried look on his face.
"It goes through all kinds of woods. How we going to
follow this?"

"They probably don't have signposts up, either,"
Jake said.

"Well, we've got to go anyway," Dave put in. "It
would have been better if we had stayed here in the
first place."

Josh took his rebuke silently. "Get your things together," he said. "Let's make sure we have all our weapons and all the food we can carry. This is going to be a rough journey."

"Well, I swan!" Reb gasped. "I never saw it rain like this." His tall cowboy hat was soaked, and water was pouring off the brim in a torrent. His shirt and jeans were sopping as were those of all the other boys.

They had been marching for two days and had made good time until the rain started. Now they were wading through mud that sucked at their feet and made the going almost impossible.

"Feels like the start of a worldwide flood," Wash gasped. His own floppy hat was pulled down over his ears, and he looked small and miserable, which he probably was.

"How we going to cook anything in this mess?" Dave complained. "We couldn't build a fire in a million years. Everything's soaking wet."

"We'll just have a cold meal and march on," Josh said.

Reb shook his head sadly. "There's not even a trail to follow anymore, Josh. This rain's washed out all the footprints. All we've got is that map."

"Well, let's follow it," Josh said. "At least we know we haven't gotten off so far. Those two twin trees there—that's one of the signs on the map that marked the trail."

Two massive trees that had grown together rose into the air before them.

"Let's keep going," he said wearily. "We can make a few more miles."

"Maybe it'll stop raining," Wash said hopefully as he trudged along beside Josh.

"I doubt it," Josh muttered.

"Don't be downhearted, Josh. We'll be all right."

"And what makes you think that?"

"Why, we always have been, haven't we?"

"Always a first time."

Wash looked over at him, and Josh was sure Wash saw the misery written on his face.

"Don't be faulting yourself because we went hunting," Wash said. "Going hunting was all right."

"Well, this part of it *is* all my fault. We should have taken the girls with us."

"'Course, if we had done that, nobody would have been home when Goél got there. He might have sent somebody else to help those Cloud folks."

"I wish he had!"

"Aw, come on, Josh! You're just wet and cold and miserable right now. We'll do fine like we always do. Goél's not let us down yet."

"It's all Sarah's fault," Josh said, abruptly changing his mind. "If she hadn't acted the way she had, we wouldn't be out here in this mess."

"Well, I don't think it was *all* Sarah's fault."

"Oh, it *was* my fault, then!"

"I think part of it was, Josh. You'd better face up to it. I expect we *were* wrong to run off and leave those girls."

Josh glared at the smaller boy but could not answer. He knew that he had been wrong, and he wished desperately that he had behaved differently. There was no going back, however, so they trudged on until darkness came.

They made a cold camp, for everything was too

wet to start a fire. Then they ate the last of their food and slept, miserable and wet, all night.

The next morning they started out at dawn. Happily, the rain had stopped, and by noon they managed to build a fire.

For lunch, Reb shot something that looked like a large turkey but had scarlet and yellow feathers. "This is bigger than any turkey I ever saw. I hope he tastes as good as turkey."

The fowl was strong tasting, but the boys were hungry, and they devoured every morsel.

All day long they trudged along. When the sun was going down, Josh checked the map one more time. "We should have come to this mountain that's on the map here. I haven't seen anything that even looks like a mountain."

"There hasn't been one," Reb said. "Nothing bigger than an anthill."

"Then we're lost," Dave said. "That's fine!"

They examined the map carefully but could not figure out where they had gone wrong.

"I don't know what to do tomorrow," Josh finally said. "Go back and start over, I guess."

Before they went to sleep that night, Jake sat beside Josh while they both stared into the small fire. "I don't know as going back would do any good," Jake said, "Why don't we forge on and hope we find another one of the landmarks—or maybe even somebody to guide us?"

"I guess we'll have to," Josh said. He felt bone tired.

The next morning they struggled through underbrush that clawed at their jeans and tore their shirts. At noon they were about to pause for a rest when suddenly Reb yelled, "Hey, look there! There's somebody up ahead!"

Eagerly Josh looked. And there came a strange appearing individual. "Let's talk to him," he said. "Maybe he can tell us how to get where we are going."

The man they approached was tall and lean with black hair and unfriendly dark eyes. He was wearing pants and a jacket made of animal skin with the smooth side turned outward. He looked sort of the way Robinson Crusoe would have looked, Josh thought.

"I'm afraid we're lost. Can you help us?"

"I don't make a living helping lost fools!"

Josh blinked but could see no reason for continuing along this line.

"Sorry to bother you," he said. "But it would be a great help if you could just tell us where we are."

"Where do you think you are?"

"I think we're lost. We're trying to get to the country of the Cloud People. Do you know the way?"

"Maybe I do, and maybe I don't."

The man seemed to be cantankerous on general principles. He stood eyeing the five boys, and finally he said, "If I were you, I wouldn't go this way."

"Why not?" Reb demanded.

"Because that's where them Earth Dwellers live, and they're bad people."

"We're not looking for any Earth Dwellers. We're looking for the Cloud People."

"Don't I know that!" the man snapped. "But you have to go through the country of the Earth Dwellers to get to the Cloud People."

"Well, then, are we headed in the right direction?" Josh asked almost in despair.

"Yep. Right into destruction. That's where you're headed."

No matter what questions they asked, the stranger—who refused to give his name—was pessimistic.

Finally Josh just spread out the map and said, "Look. If you'll just show us where we are and which way to go to get to the Cloud People, we'd appreciate it."

"Some people ain't got no sense," the man muttered. He put a dirty finger on the map and said, "You're right here."

"And where are the Cloud People?"

"The map's wrong," the man grunted. "It ought to be over here. But you'll never make it through the Earth Dwellers' territory anyhow."

"So we just follow this river until we get to this mountain and turn left and head through this country?"

"That's right. But you won't make it."

"Thanks a lot. Always good to have a cheerful word," Jake said. "I hope you have a good day."

The man glared at him and stalked off.

"Little Mr. Sunshine, isn't he?" Dave said with a scowl. "You think he knows what he's talking about?"

"I guess he does," Jake said slowly. "And he doesn't think very highly of the Earth Dwellers."

"Well, according to this map, there's no other way to get to the country of the Cloud People," Josh said. "So we might as well get at it."

All the next day, the five boys struggled to keep up a pace that often left Wash gasping for breath. Reb was the scout. He would disappear, running ahead, and then come back saying, "It's OK up ahead. Don't see anything scary."

"It's a good thing Reb's such a good scout," Josh said to Jake as they fought to keep up.

"He never seems to get tired. I wish I could run like he can."

"How much farther do you think it is?" Dave asked. "We're going to wear our feet off to the ankles."

They had seen no sign of people at all, and Wash said once, "This is sure a desolate part of the country."

"According to this map, I think we're in the ancient forest," Josh said. He looked up at the enormous trees and wondered at the size of them. "I never saw such big trees!"

When it was nearly dark again, Josh said, "We'd better stop and make camp. It'll be dark in thirty minutes."

"Wash and I'll get some firewood," Dave offered.

"I'll go out and see if I can quick bring down something to eat," Reb said. "Maybe another one of them red turkeys."

He left at once. The others lay out their sleeping bags and then made a fire. Reb came back after a while bearing a small piglike animal. Little as it was, it had the sharpest, longest tusk any of them had ever seen.

"This is just a young one, I reckon," Reb said. "He'll be good and tender." He plunked the body down and had pulled out his knife when suddenly Wash yelled, "Look out!"

Reb whirled. What appeared to be a whole herd of wild pigs was rushing from among the trees. Some of them were as big as Shetland ponies. "Quick! Up in the tree!" he yelled. "We can't fight that many!"

It was a very close thing. The boys scrambled up into the branches as the pigs, now squealing with anger, tried to get at them.

"Good thing those things can't climb trees," Jake said. He sounded out of breath from the effort. "Look at that. They're tearing up our stuff."

"Well, I'll stop their clock!" Reb said. He had his quiver over his back. The rest of them sat in the branches with no weapons at all. Reb drew the bow back and sent an arrow that struck one of the pigs directly in the chest. There was a wild squealing in the herd, as the animal fell over.

"Drive 'em off, Reb," Josh yelled.

Reb Jackson continued to shoot. Although he did not kill any more, he struck enough in the flanks and in the shoulders that finally, with furious squeals, the herd drew away into the forest.

"You reckon they're gone?"

"I hope so," Wash said. "I never saw such pigs."

After a short wait, the boys scrambled down from the tree, and Reb stood over the monster he had shot.

"Well, we're gonna have bacon and ham tonight."

Josh stood staring down at the enormous beast with teeth like white swords. His heart was still beating fast.

"If that's a sample of what they've got in the ancient forest, I'd just as soon not have any," Reb said finally. "They almost got us."

"They sure did," Josh said. "And that tells me we'd better not sleep on the ground tonight."

So it was that the Sleepers clung to branches all night long. There was little sleep, and Josh kept wondering what the ancient forest would yield on the next day. He was still conscience stricken too, thinking their trouble was really all his fault. Finally he did drift off, and he dreamed of Sarah Collingwood and how he would apologize when he saw her again.

8
Sarah Gets Some Help

In a short time, Abbey had grown close to Prince Jere. She was always attracted to a good-looking boy, anyway, and, although he was several years older, she was flattered by the way he paid attention to her. She had discovered he was a good singer, and she loved to listen to him. As for his poems, she was not a judge of that, for she knew little about poetry.

The two of them sat on a platform that jutted out from the king's castle. Below, the earth seemed very far away, and above was the pleasant sound of wind blowing through the trees. Jere had just finished singing a song, and he grinned at her. "How did you like that one?"

"I liked the song fine, Prince Jere. You're a marvelous singer."

"I wrote the words myself," he informed her.

"Well, I spent a lot of time listening to CDs back in OldWorld."

"What's a Cee Dee?"

"Oh, it's a kind of music that's canned."

"How can music be canned?"

Abbey spent some time explaining the miracles of CDs and recordings to Jere. He was fascinated. "I wish there was such a thing as a Cee Dee here," he said. "Then I could put all my songs on it, and everyone could listen."

"You'd be a star."

"A star?" Prince Jere looked toward the sky.

"Oh, that's what they called musicians who were very popular. Stars."

"Prince Jere, the star. Here. Let me sing you another one."

The prince sang another song, and then Abbey said, "Most of the songs back in OldWorld were about love."

"Really?"

"Oh yes. About boys falling in love with girls. And courting them."

"What's that?"

Abbey began explaining. She had already explained courtship more than once to Enid, who could not seem to get the concept into her head.

Jere listened, but he said, "Well, that would be great for us poets and songwriters, but I don't think most men around here would like it."

"I guess they wouldn't. The men have made slaves out of all the women."

"No, that's not so," Jere protested. "If you want to see slaves, you ought to go to the Earth Dwellers. They *really* make slaves out of people."

"But, Prince, the men here just don't treat women right," Abbey protested.

The discussion that followed lasted for nearly an hour. Finally Abbey just threw up her hands in despair. "It's like trying to explain colors to a blind person!" she said with exasperation. "Can't you understand that women and men are of the same importance."

"But they're not," Jere said. "Men are stronger than females. And can climb vines faster."

"That's true. But women are gentler. They're just as smart."

"You would have a hard time convincing the Cloud People about that."

"You know what you'd do if you were a real man, Jere?"

"Now what do you mean—if I were a 'real man'?"

"I mean your father thinks all you can do is sing songs and write poetry."

Jere's face fell. "Well, you're right about that," he admitted.

"Then why don't you show him you can do more?"

"And how could I do that?"

"It's easy. Sarah's getting ready to go and face the chief of the Earth Dwellers. What's his name?"

"His name is Maroni."

"If you want to show what a man you are—braver than a girl—you'll go with her."

"My father would never agree to that."

"You see? You're so afraid of what your father would say, you won't talk to him about doing what's right. You know Sarah needs help."

"But it's a foolish thing she's doing!"

"I'm telling you, Prince Jere, I've seen some strange things. But Goél always helped us." Abbey went on to tell some of the adventures the Seven Sleepers had had. She finished by saying, "So this is a chance to prove you're a man."

Prince Jere just shook his head doubtfully.

When the prince left Abbey, he stayed by himself for some time, thinking about what she had said. Finally he decided, *She may be right.*

He walked into the throne room, where his father was speaking with Sarah.

"I'm trying for the last time to tell you that this is foolish!"

"I'm sorry, sire," Sarah said. "But this is one time I must displease you."

"Well, you're not one of my subjects. You are one of the Sleepers. I suppose I will have to let you go." But he looked doubtful. "I wish the men would get here."

"I'll be all right, sire."

"Yes, she will," Jere said suddenly. He stepped up beside Sarah and added, "I have decided to go with her, Father."

And that was the beginning of a violent disagreement.

With an amazed look on her face, Sarah stood back and watched the two argue loudly. She no doubt had guessed that this was the first time Jere had ever offered to do anything but write poetry.

"I'm telling you it's suicide!" the king shouted. "You know what those Earth Dwellers are like, Jere!"

But Jere had thrown himself into this idea with all of his might. "If a girl can face them, I can, too. I can't let a female outdo me, can I?"

The king sputtered. "That's different."

"Not very," Jere said. "Father, I promise that we'll just look the situation over to see what can be done to free the captives. We won't do anything foolish. I don't think you'll be disappointed."

Celevorn tried his best, but his son was adamant. Finally the king said sadly, "I'm glad to see you taking an interest in the affairs of the kingdom. But I wish you'd be more sensible."

Then Sarah spoke up. "I think the prince is showing signs of real maturity, King Celevorn."

Celevorn eyed his son, and hope came into his eyes. "Son," he said, "you know you're all I have left. I wouldn't want anything to happen to you. But I agree. You may go. Be careful."

"We'll be all right. You'll see."

Sarah and Prince Jere left the next day at dawn. Everyone had gathered, it seemed, to watch the pair leave.

Farewells were said, and Abbey clung to Sarah, suddenly changing her mind and begging her not to go. "Just wait for the guys to get here," she pleaded.

"No, I've made up my mind," Sarah said firmly. "It will be fine. By the time they get here, Jere and I may have settled it all. You just wait here."

Jere embraced the king, saying, "Don't worry, Father. It'll be all right."

Sarah got into the basket and clung to it, her eyes shut. Jere slid down on a vine.

As soon as they reached the ground, Sarah got out and drew a deep breath. "It feels good to have the earth under my feet again."

"Not me," Jere said, looking around nervously. "I feel a lot better up in our city."

"Well, to each his own," Sarah said. "But we'd better get going right away. Which way is it?"

"We'll go this way." He pointed.

Jere had his staff in hand, and a knife was in his belt. Sarah kept an arrow notched, ready for whatever might come.

They made their way quickly, and after a while Sarah asked, "How much farther is it?"

"I believe only a few miles," Jere answered.

The two had not gone more than a mile farther when Sarah saw a young woman running through the woods toward them. Terror was written on her face.

"Look at that girl. Something must be after her," Sarah cried.

Almost as soon as she had spoken, a giant scorpion scuttled into view behind the girl.

Sarah reached for her bow.

The girl stumbled toward them, her eyes blank with fright. "Help me!" she cried.

At that moment another scorpion emerged from the woods. Sarah's lips tightened. "I can't get both of them, Jere!"

"I'll take the second one." Raising his staff like a club, Jere ran toward the awful looking spotted beast.

The first scorpion lunged toward Sarah, and she loosed an arrow. It took the scorpion in the body, and the beast uttered a wild screech. Quickly she notched another, and it struck the creature also.

By that time she saw that the second scorpion had reached Jere. He stood tall and straight, ready to use the staff like a baseball bat. The scorpion charged at him, its terrible stinger poised.

Jere had timed it exactly right. He struck the stinger before it struck him—and with such force that the stinger broke away from the scorpion's tail.

Again there was a wild screech, and for a time the beast repeatedly tried to bite Jere with its serpentlike head.

The scorpion lunged, but Jere fended it off. Finally he struck it a mighty blow to the head. There was a crunching, and the beast fell to the ground with all six legs kicking.

"You've got him, Prince! Wonderful!"

Jere turned toward her, his chest heaving. "I never would have thought I could do that," he gasped. "And I never saw anyone shoot an arrow like you do."

"Who are you?"

Both turned to the young woman they had rescued. She had large, dark eyes, and they were open wide.

"My name is Prince Jere of the Cloud People. What is your name?"

"I am Lomeen. And I thank you both for what you did."

"Are you perhaps one of the Earth Dwellers?" Sarah asked.

"Yes. My father is Maroni, the chief."

Sarah's heart leaped. *What a break!* she thought. *To save the daughter of the chief. That ought to help.*

She said quickly, "My name is Sarah. I am one of the Seven Sleepers. Have you ever heard of us?"

Lomeen's eyes grew even larger. "My mother used to speak of the Seven Sleepers often, but she died. Since then, we have not heard of them."

"We've come to talk to your father," Sarah said. "Will you take us there?"

"Of course. Come this way."

An hour later, Lomeen brought Sarah and the prince into the Earth Dwellers' village. For the most part, it was made of mud huts with branches for covering. In one such structure she found the chief.

"This is my father, Chief Maroni. Father, this young man and this young woman saved my life." She related how the two of them had killed the scorpions, and now the chief's eyes grew large. "No one has ever killed a scorpion singlehanded with just a staff," he said.

"He was *very* brave, Father," Lomeen said.

Maroni was thoughtful for a moment and then nodded. "We are grateful."

"*Who are these strangers?*" A little man wearing

the teeth of animals made into a necklace stood in the doorway. He had fierce eyes, and, though he was small, everyone backed away from him immediately.

"This is Nomus, the high priest," the chief said.

Sarah knew immediately that she was facing the enemy. But she looked long into the eyes of the high priest of Nimbo and did not flinch.

"Chief," she said, turning back to him, "we have been sent by Goél."

Nomus screamed. "*Goél!* We will have none of *his* people here!"

Maroni seemed stunned. Grateful as he probably was to the young strangers, obviously he was intimidated by Nomus.

Sarah saw that the battle would be fought on these grounds. "Chief, we come in peace, and we come to help your people."

Maroni gazed at her. Then, surprisingly ignoring the protests of Nomus, he said, "We will hear you. You are welcome to our village."

9

The Priest's Decision

Sarah walked along with Lomeen. On the other side of the chief's daughter was Jere, accompanying them. Lomeen had offered to show them around the village of the Earth Dwellers and was pointing out what sights there were to see. In truth, there was not much. The village was not an attractive place, and there were few signs of wealth.

"That is where my father, the chief, lives," Lomeen said, indicating a larger house built of earth.

Trying to think of something nice to say about the homely structure, Sarah said, "It looks very strong."

"Oh yes. We build our houses well. We put straw and rocks into the red mud that we find along the riverbank. When it dries, it is so hard that no spear can penetrate it. Would you care to see inside?"

"Why, yes. We'd like that very much. Wouldn't we, Jere?"

"Yes, indeed!"

Actually Jere had recently whispered that he was rather depressed by the village. He was used to light, airy structures, and these houses were all heavy with few windows. He wondered how anybody could live in such a place. The whole village was surrounded by heavy jungle, and there was little attractiveness about it anywhere.

"Come in," Lomeen said, stepping through the doorway, which was covered by an animal hide of some kind. She waited until the two had entered. "This is the main room," she said rather shyly.

The room was some fifteen feet square, and what furniture there was was made of wood. Sarah went to a chair that was beautifully carved and said, "This is a fine chair, Lomeen. Who made this?"

"My father and I made it. We like to make things together. The wood is very hard, so it took a long time."

"You're quite an artist," Jere said, coming over to admire the chair. It was a beautiful piece of furniture, indeed, curved to fit the body and making one long to sit in it. "Mind if I try it?"

"Oh, please do!" Lomeen said quickly.

Jere sat down and stretched luxuriously. "It's so comfortable," he said. "It's hard to believe that anything as hard as this could be comfortable."

"We made all the furniture in here. All of my people are good woodcarvers."

They looked at each table and individual chair. No two were alike, and the woods varied all the way from having a dark walnut look to wood that was almost white.

"We don't have anything like this where I live." Jere smiled at the girl.

She flushed and looked down at the floor. "I can't see how you could live up in the clouds," she said.

"Well, I suppose it's all what a person's brought up to. You ought to come for a visit sometime."

"Oh no! I could never do that! My father would never allow it."

Jere exchanged a glance with Sarah, and then he asked, "Why not, Lomeen?"

"Because our two peoples are separated. You know that, Prince Jere."

He shrugged his broad shoulders. "I know that is so, but to be enemies is wrong. I do not see *why* we have to be enemies."

"That's right," Sarah said quickly. "Your two tribes ought to live together in peace."

"That is what I would like," Lomeen said eagerly. She was an attractive girl, and her smile came quickly. She shot a quick look at Jere and asked, "Are the rest of your people like you?"

"Like me? Well, I suppose so. Except my father doesn't look with favor on me. He thinks I waste too much time singing songs and writing poems."

"You make up poems? I'd love to hear them."

Jere laughed quickly. "Well, you don't have to beg a poet for a demonstration. Here is one that I made up on the way over here."

When he had recited it, Lomeen said, "Why, that is beautiful! Do you have many others like that?"

"Quite a few. But as I say, my father would rather I would be more practical."

They talked eagerly, and Sarah listened, hiding a smile.

Then they all went outside, where they were met by one of the tribesmen, who said at once, "The strangers are wanted at the Council of the Elders."

The man led them through the village until they came to an open field. There, it seemed, most of the villagers had gathered. They looked curiously at Sarah and Jere, some of the men with unfriendly faces. Sarah saw Chief Maroni and Nomus, the high priest, standing by themselves. The priest scowled as they approached.

But the chief smiled warmly at his daughter. He seemed to have a special love for her, Sarah noted. She noted also that the chief's eyes went to Jere with a rather curious expression. However, he said only, "We have gathered together to hear what the strangers have to say."

Nomus suddenly said very loudly, "We do not need to know what they have to say! They are our prisoners!"

"These strangers saved my life!" Lomeen said. "The man killed a scorpion with nothing but a staff. To save me."

A murmur went around the crowd, and looks of admiration began to appear on the faces of some of the villagers.

"Nothing but a staff," Maroni said. "Yes, that is admirable indeed!"

But a large, rough looking man who stood close by said, "I do not believe it!"

"This is Chan, Chief of Warriors," the chief said. "Why do you not believe it, Chan? My daughter is here and safe."

The warrior chief said, "Because it is impossible. No one could kill a scorpion by himself. It takes several warriors, well armed, to kill one of those beasts!"

"Nevertheless, he did it. I saw him. And Sarah, the Sleeper, killed one with a single arrow."

Another murmur went around the crowd.

Sarah felt that it was time for her to speak up. "Chan, I'm sorry you do not believe what the chief's daughter has said. But it is true. You will find the bodies of the scorpions where we left them."

"That is fair enough," Maroni said. He nodded to a warrior. "Go back along the trail and return with a report."

As soon as the warrior left at a dead run, the chief said, "Now, why have you come? Especially you, Jere,

88

son of Celevorn. You know our two tribes are enemies."

"I came to accompany this young woman, Chief," Jere said. "She is a stranger to our world, and I thought to offer her my protection."

"You are foolish to come into our camp! You will never leave here alive!" Nomus snarled.

"Some of you here, perhaps, have heard of Goél," Sarah said. Her eyes flickered over the audience, and she saw recognition come. "I understand that Lomeen's mother was a believer in Goél."

"That is true," the chief said. "She was a good woman, and I still miss her to this day."

"She was also a very wise woman if she believed in Goél. He is good and strong and powerful. And he has sent us to this place to bring your senseless fighting to a stop."

"You speak of Goél!" Nomus said loudly, a sneer on his face. "Where is this famous Goél?"

"He is not here, but he has sent us, his messengers. Some of you have also heard of the Seven Sleepers. Have you not?"

"We have heard tales of the Sleepers," Maroni said. He looked long at Sarah. "We would expect more than a young female, though."

"The race is not always to the swift or the battle to the strong, Chief Maroni," Sarah said. "It is wisdom that is needed. Not more killing. You surely see how wrong it is for you to slay your neighbors."

Nomus cried out, "We will hear no more of this!"

"Wait!" Chief Maroni said. "Let the stranger speak!"

"Thank you, Chief. Just imagine that *you* had an enemy that captured your wives and your children and put them to death. Would that please you? Of course not! And there is no reason why you should be doing such a thing. The Cloud People are harmless. They would never harm any of your people."

"That's not so!" Nomus cried. "They have killed several of our warriors."

"Only in self-defense," Jere said. "We never come to your villages looking for victims." His eyes flashed as he looked about. "Is it not the Earth Dwellers who come seeking victims among my people?"

"Be quiet, boy!" Nomus said. "You are no warrior! I can see that!"

"Let me kill him where he stands!" Chan growled.

Sarah swiftly notched an arrow and aimed it at the Chief Warrior's breast. "Stop where you are, Chan! If you move one more step, you will have an arrow in your heart!"

Chan appeared shocked at the speed with which she had moved. He stood still and grew pale.

Sarah smiled. "All I have to do is let loose this arrow, and you will be a dead man. Would that please you, Chief Maroni?"

"No!" Maroni said quickly. "Of course not."

"Neither does it please Celevorn when your warriors take the lives of his people." Sarah relaxed the pressure on the bowstring, and Chan took a deep breath. She kept the bow in her hands, however, not knowing what the brutal man would do.

"Nimbo must have victims," Nomus shouted. "He demands it. If he does not get them, our crops will not grow. Our people will die."

"That is not true!" Sarah said. "You have no proof of all this."

Nomus at once began crying out that their god, Nimbo, must have blood.

Sarah let him rave. She had seen immediately that the priest was the trouble. Obviously Chief Maroni was a good, though weak, man. He had kindness in his face, but she saw also that he was dominated by Nomus. Now she lifted her bow again and pointed an arrow directly at the priest. "Now, *your* life is in my hands, Nomus. If I loose my fingers, can you dodge an arrow? No, you would die."

Nomus stood very still. "Wait," he said. "Do not kill me."

"Why not? You are responsible for the deaths of many. Suppose I should tell you that Goél demands a sacrifice?"

Nomus's throat worked convulsively, and no one said a word.

Lomeen was watching closely, probably hoping Sarah would loose the arrow. Sarah knew the girl hated Nomus, as did many of the villagers. Lomeen would not have grieved, for he was a cruel and ruthless murderer.

"Do not kill him, O Sleeper," Chief Maroni said quickly.

"I will not, Chief," Sarah said. "But I will point out that it would be very easy for me to do so. It is easy to take life, but who can give it back?"

"That is right, Chief," Jere said. "Life is a precious thing. It is like water that a man holds in his hands. When he lets it go to the earth, who could gather it back again?"

Jere spoke eloquently for a time, and Chief Maroni and his people listened quietly. Sarah herself was surprised at how well Jere spoke. She saw also that Lomeen kept watching him.

Finally Chief Maroni held up a hand. "We will discuss what you say, my council and I, and we will talk again. Meantime, you will be our guests. Now let us have no more talk of killing."

As the crowd broke up, Lomeen walked up to Jere. "Would you like to see more of the village?" she asked rather shyly.

"I would."

"And will you tell me some more of your poems?"

He laughed. His teeth were white against his tanned skin, making him very handsome, Sarah thought. "You ask a poet that? I'll quote poetry until your ears fall off. I sing too. Did you know that?"

"No! Will you sing some of your poems for me?"

Jere smiled with satisfaction. "You show me the village, and I'll recite some of my best poems."

Lomeen and the two strangers walked away, and Chief Maroni watched them go. A thought came to his mind, but he shook his head. He was becoming very troubled about some of the things that were happening. Deep down, he felt that Nomus had great powers. Perhaps evil powers.

It was half an hour later when Nomus appeared at the chief's home. Coming in, he at once said, "You must not let this young man and this silly Sleeper sway you, O Chief."

"But she did not seem silly to me, Nomus. And you did not think so when she held an arrow pointed at your heart."

Anger caused Nomus's face to flush. "She is an enemy sent to destroy us! She wants to destroy the confidence the people have in Nimbo."

Chief Maroni listened as the priest spoke harshly for a long time against the young man and the Sleeper.

But ultimately the chief gathered up his courage and said, "I will hear no more of this, Nomus."

The high priest appeared astonished. His power, until now, had been unchallenged. Until now, he had had complete influence over Chief Maroni. He swallowed hard, biting back any angry words that leaped to his lips. He said, "You will see. If these two are allowed to have their way, Nimbo will be angry, and we will pay!"

"Yes, we will see," the chief said. "Now you may go."

Nomus left the chief's house, his heart boiling with anger. He was met almost at once by Chan.

"What did he say?" Chan asked.

Reluctantly Nomus said, "He is under the sway of those two strangers. I think the girl is a witch."

"What will you do?"

Nomus stopped dead still, and anger flashed in his eyes. He looked into the brutal face of Chan, the killer warrior, and whispered, "They must die! Both of them!"

10

Bad News

I never saw anything like this in all my life!" Reb said in almost a whisper. "Look at the size of these trees! I wouldn't have thought such a thing was possible!"

Josh was equally stunned. But they were somewhere in the country of the Cloud People. There was little doubt of that.

Dave looked up, straining his eyes. "Think what the timber companies back home could have done with these monsters. They make the giant sequoias in California look like bushes."

Jake and Wash were staring upward, too. Jake was muttering in disbelief. "I remember what the fellow said when he saw his first camel."

"What did he say, Jake?" Wash said.

"He said, 'There ain't no such animal.' I'm almost tempted to say there ain't no trees this big!"

"Anyway, I think we've come to the right place according to what the man said and according to Sarah's map," Josh said.

"That's well enough. But what do we do now?" Dave said, a puzzled look on his face. "This forest could go on for miles, and the girls could be anywhere."

"Too bad we got off the trail back there," Reb said. "Maybe we ought to just spread out and start calling them."

"We'd get lost in a minute that way," Josh said. "We'd better stick together."

He thought Reb looked unhappy with this decision, but the Southerner said no more. He knew how to find his way almost anywhere, of course. But he was also aware that others, such as Jake, could get lost in their own bedroom.

So they just kept on wandering through the forest. Everybody kept watching for wild animals, but they saw no signs of any. "I'll bet it's a rough place here at night, though," Josh said. "No telling what kind of wild beasts are around here."

They walked until they grew hungry. They had a little food left—the remains of a small deer that Dave had brought down—and they sat down and finished it. They were still hungry.

A beautiful stream cut its way between the trees, and Reb said, "I bet there's fish in there. See? There's one broke water."

"What do you say we put out some lines?" Wash asked. "We've got to have something more to eat."

But Josh said, "We don't have time to fish." He was impatient and worried as well. He still felt that he had made a mistake by going off and leaving the two girls alone, and now he was more uneasy than he cared to show.

However, Reb said, "Tell you what. Let's do split up. You fellows stay here and catch some fish. I'll go on and scout. I'll bet I can find something—although I haven't seen any tracks yet."

Josh shrugged. "That may be the best idea, Reb. You're a good tracker. We'll try to catch enough fish to feed us for right now. And then when you get back, maybe you'll have something else."

Reb took off, and the other boys all got out the fishing lines they always carried. The stream seemed full of fish. They were small silver-colored ones with red streaks on their backs, and Wash smacked his lips. "I bet these will make good eating!"

As soon as they had caught enough, Jake and Josh cleaned them, and by the time they were cooking, Reb came back.

"Did you find anything?" Josh asked eagerly.

"Nothing but more big trees and one of the biggest bugs you ever saw. Just like a scorpion only big as a horse."

"Did you kill it?"

"Not much," Reb grinned. He shoved his Stetson back on his forehead and said, "If I'd had my old 30-30 from home, I'll bet I could have cleaned his plow."

"Sit down and have some of this fish. They're real good," Wash told him.

As the boys finished eating, Josh said, "I've been thinking about something. Every village we've ever seen anywhere was always set close to water. I think we ought to follow this stream."

"That's not a bad idea, Josh," Dave Cooper said. "Primitive societies always got close to the water if they could. If we follow the brook, we may come to something."

"Then let's get at it. We haven't got much more daylight," Reb said.

The boys packed their gear, including enough cooked fish to feed them for supper. Then they followed the stream, which was very simple to do since there was little undergrowth.

"I never saw any country like this," Reb said again. "It's real odd. Giant trees, but there's no undergrowth down here."

"I don't think there's enough sun," Josh said. "It

looks kind of like the Amazon rain forest. I've seen pictures of places where the branches just blocked out the sun."

The boys made their way along the bank, from time to time shouting for the girls. Then they stopped for a break, bending over and drinking water out of their cupped hands.

And then Reb suddenly said quietly, "*Ssh!* Listen to that."

"What is it, Reb?" Wash whispered.

"Listen!"

Josh listened with all of his might. He knew Reb's hearing was better than most, but finally he said, "I hear it, too. It's somebody calling."

"I can't hear a thing," Dave said, glancing around. "I don't see anybody, either."

Reb looked up. "It's coming from up there!"

"From the *tree?* Well, give 'em a hail, Reb," Josh said. "You can holler louder than anybody."

Reb cupped his hands and shouted upward. "Is there anybody up there?"

"Reb, it's me—Abbey!"

Everyone heard the faint voice this time, and Josh said happily, "We've found them! Where are you, Abbey?" he shouted.

"Stay right there!" the faraway voice called back, and in a few moments the boys were astonished to see empty baskets coming down from the tree, each tied to a stout vine.

There was also a single vine down which a young man slid. He came to the ground and nodded a greeting. "My name is Teanor," he said. "I assume you are the warriors called the Sleepers."

"That's right. I'm Josh Adams," Josh said. "Are Sarah and Abbey up there?"

"Abbey is."

"Where's Sarah?" Josh demanded.

"I will let our king do the talking. Get into the baskets."

Josh looked at a basket and shook his head. "I never did like high places."

"Well, you're sure not gonna *climb* that tree," Reb said. "Get in. Just shut your eyes."

The boys got into the baskets, and they began slowly rising. Josh held on until his fingers turned white. Reb, in a nearby basket, said, "Better open up your eyes, Josh. It's quite a sight."

Josh sensed the ground was slowly falling away. He grimly held on, but he did open his eyes. His basket ascended in fits and jerks. Up—up—up it went, and Josh whispered, "I hope I don't get airsick."

"This is some elevator ride, isn't it, now?" Wash asked from his basket.

Jake must have looked at the vine then and decided it was too feeble to hold his weight. "I sure hope that vine doesn't break," he said. "It doesn't look too strong to me."

"It won't break," Josh heard Teanor say. "I helped make these lifts myself." The young man was climbing up his vine steadily and quite easily, the muscles in his shoulders working like cables.

"Just look at him go!" Wash said as now Teanor climbed away from them. "He can climb quicker than any monkey I ever saw."

Finally the baskets reached a kind of deck, and Josh gave a deep sigh of relief as he stepped off. The platform was made of saplings and seemed rather flimsy, but it was much more stable than the basket. He moved quickly away from the edge, saying, "I wish there were some rails."

"What are rails?" Teanor asked with a puzzled expression.

"Something built to keep you from falling off."

Teanor laughed. "Why should you fall off? That would be foolish."

Reb himself did not particularly care for high places, and he too stayed back from the edge. "Doesn't anybody ever fall off?"

"Not very often," Teanor said carelessly. "Maybe old people or maybe a female once in a while."

"Who is your leader here, Teanor?"

"King Celevorn. I will take you to him."

Even as he turned, Abbey came flying across a swinging bridge from another platform. "Josh—Dave!" she cried. She hugged each of them and then Wash and Jake and Reb. "I'm so glad to see you!" Her eyes were shining, and she could hardly talk. "How did you ever find us?"

"It wasn't easy," Josh said. He looked around. "But where is Sarah?"

"She's not here. She's gone on a mission."

"What kind of a mission?" Josh cried.

Abbey hesitated. "Well, it's a long story."

"You can tell it in front of the king," Teanor said. "Please. He's anxious to see the male Sleepers. I'll take you to him."

There was little choice, so the six of them followed Teanor. Getting across the rather flimsy bridges was an unwelcome chore for those who did not like high places. Josh didn't enjoy them. Wash had never been afraid of heights, and he merely walked across as if they were solid concrete sidewalks. Jake, however, crept on his hands and knees across one particularly fragile looking structure.

"Might as well stop crawling around, Jake," Wash said.

"You cross the bridges like you want to, and I'll do it my way!" Jake replied.

When they reached the most imposing looking of the houses, Teanor said, "This is the home of King Celevorn. Come in. The king is eager to see you."

The six entered, and Josh knew at once that he was looking at a kingly man. Celevorn was seated on his throne, but he got up and said, "Welcome to the Sleepers. We are glad you have arrived safely."

"Thank you, King Celevorn," Josh said. "My name is Josh Adams, and these are my friends." He introduced the others, then said, "We are anxious about our friend Sarah."

"Well might you be," Celevorn said grimly. "She has gone on a very foolish mission."

"Tell me about it, please!" Josh said worriedly. "We are very concerned about her." He listened as the king explained the feud that was going on between the Earth Dwellers and the Cloud People. He related that Sarah had decided to go and seek the release of one of his people. He ended by saying, "If she chose to go, that was her business. But my son went with her, and that is my business!"

"How long ago was this?" Josh demanded.

"It was two days ago."

"And you've heard nothing?"

"No. And now I must hear your plan. It is well known that the Sleepers bring help to people that are oppressed. Tell me what it is we are to do."

Josh's mouth dropped open. "But, Your Majesty, I just got here."

"I have told you the problem," King Celevorn said. "I am concerned about my son. And you should be concerned about your friend Sarah."

"They are probably dead by now," Teanor muttered. "They shouldn't have gone."

Josh's heart sank. "We will have to go at once to find them."

"You cannot go now. It is too late in the day. There are fierce beasts below," the king said.

Josh, if he'd had his own way, would have rushed off to rescue Sarah, anyway. But Reb said, "The king is right, Josh. We got to show a little wisdom here. Now, let's find out all we can about these Earth Dwellers."

The king said, "We will have food prepared. We will talk as we eat."

The meal was very good—it consisted of vegetables and fresh meat and fish. As it began, Josh looked around and did not see Abbey. "Where's Abbey?" he asked.

"The female? She's eating with the other women."

"Oh, men do not eat with women in this place?" Dave said. Surprise and then displeasure showed on his face.

King Celevorn eyed him. "We have heard some of your ideas from the two females. They tell us that women have great rights in the place where you live. It is not so here."

Josh saw the girl Enid, who was serving, look up quickly. She met the eyes of Teanor, and he managed a faint smile.

Conversation went on around the table for some time, and then Josh and the others were led to their quarters. The boys were placed in one tree house large enough for all of them, so before they went to sleep they sat and talked about the situation.

Josh said, "This is a fine mess! I'm worried about Sarah."

"We'll just have to hope she's all right," Jake said quickly.

"Teanor doesn't think so," Josh said glumly. "These Earth Dwellers must be a vicious bunch."

"Well, we can't do anything tonight," Wash said. "The best thing we can do is get a good night's sleep."

They were all exhausted from their long trip. Even Josh fell asleep almost at once.

The next morning, Abbey met them as they left their house. "Bad news," she said. "A messenger just came back. King Celevorn sent someone to see if they could find any trace of his son and Sarah."

"And did they find them?" Josh asked. But he saw Abbey's face was filled with apprehension.

"They found them all right. He's a good scout. The best among the Cloud People."

"Well, *tell* us, Abbey! For crying out loud!" Wash cried. "What about them?"

"We're not sure, but it looks like they are being held prisoner by the Earth Dwellers."

"What does that mean?" Dave asked.

"It means," Abbey said, "they're liable to be sacrificed to the Earth Dwellers' god. That's what it means."

Shock ran through Josh Adams. He was very close to Sarah Collingwood. He knew that their priority had to be to set her free. He also saw that if they could help the king's son, it might give them better access to King Celevorn.

"We've got to do something quick," he said.

103

"It's not going to be easy," Abbey said. "I've been listening a lot since Sarah and I came here, and the Earth Dwellers are under the power of a high priest named Nomus. The king there has absolute confidence in him, and I'm afraid for Sarah and for the king's son."

Josh Adam's lips grew thin. "We'll do something," he promised. "I don't know what yet, but we'll do something."

11

The Miracle Shot

Sarah found herself becoming more and more attached to Lomeen, the daughter of Chief Maroni. Lomeen had no brothers or sisters and seemed to be a very lonely girl. The two of them spent much time together.

One day Sarah was helping Lomeen grind corn. It was a very primitive operation. The total machinery consisted of a large stone that had been hollowed out and a smaller, round stone that could be held in the hand. She watched Lomeen put a handful of corn in the hollow and then pound it with the small rock until she had made cornmeal.

"It would be nice if you had a mill, Lomeen."

"What is a mill?"

"Oh, it's a machine that grinds corn up into small bits. You can even make flour out of it."

"What is flour?"

Sarah laughed and picked up some of the fragments. "This is what we'd call cornmeal, but if you kept grinding it, you'd get corn flour. Very good to cook with."

Lomeen listened as Sarah described a grain mill. Then she sighed. "We don't have anything like that."

"I'll tell you what would be good, if you've never tried it," Sarah said.

"What is that, Sarah?"

"We'll make hominy and then grits."

Lomeen, of course, had no idea of what either hominy or grits was.

Sarah decided to teach her. She had learned on her uncle's farm back in OldWorld. The first thing she did was to put a hole in the bottom of an old wooden churn and fill the churn with wood ashes. She then poured water on top of the ashes. When the fluid came out the bottom, she said, "This is what we call lye water, Lomeen."

The girl was watching closely. "What do you do with it?"

"I will show you. It will take a while, though."

Sarah took the lye water and poured it over grains of corn to soak them. The next day, she said, "See. The corn has swelled up."

Lomeen looked at it. "It *is* big. What do you do now?"

"This is what is called hominy. What we'll do is dry some of this, and we'll eat the rest."

The hominy dish was tested by the chief himself at his table where Lomeen served him. His eyes opened wide, and he said, "This new food is good!"

"Wait'll you taste grits, Chief." Sarah grinned. "I guarantee you'll love them."

When the hominy was dry enough, Sarah pounded it into smaller fragments. It broke apart easily. When she had a plentiful supply, she said, "Now, this is grits, Lomeen. You can boil it, put some butter and salt and pepper on it, and you've got something good to eat."

"What's pepper?" Lomeen asked innocently.

Sarah gaped at her. "Well, it's something that adds flavor to food."

The grits also proved to be a success, and soon Sarah had her hands full teaching all the women how to make the two delicacies. Apparently the villagers' diet was so monotonous that anything new was a treat.

Lomeen seemed very curious about Jere. She asked Sarah innumerable questions about the young man, including one that Sarah expected.

"Does he have a wife, Sarah?"

"I don't think so."

"He is so handsome. It's a shame our people are at war."

Sarah shot a quick glance at her. "I don't think *their* people are. I think *your* people are at war. The Cloud People are very gentle. I wish you could spend a few days with Jere's people. You'd like them, Lomeen."

"Really! Do you think they'd like me?"

"Who wouldn't like you?" Sarah smiled. She proceeded to tell Lomeen as much as she could about the king's son, including the fact that he and his father did not get along well. "King Celevorn is a practical sort of man. He thinks his son ought to be busy doing important things, but Jere only wants to write poetry. He has a great imagination."

"I don't think any of our people write poetry. They wouldn't see any good in it. 'You can't eat it,' they would say."

"That's true, but there are a lot of things in life that you can't eat or use, and yet they are nice."

Jere spent some time with the two girls. He always seemed jolly and could make up little poems as easily as other people could talk. It amazed Sarah and appeared to absolutely astound Lomeen, who said she'd never heard anything like this.

The chief found the young stranger Jere quite interesting. One day the two of them went hunting, at which Jere said he was not the best in the world. He finally said, "I don't wonder that your father is displeased with you, Jere." He had heard much of this from the young man himself. "A man has to go out and bring in game."

"That's true, Chief," Jere said. "I feel ashamed of myself sometimes, but it gets so boring doing nothing but hunting—and taking care of things."

"But would you let things take care of themselves?" Maroni asked sternly. He really liked Jere, but he thought he saw a character fault here. He had talked to the young man more than once about the need for men to take charge and do things and accomplish important feats. He himself was a mighty hunter and noted among his people. Yes, the young man needed to do something important.

One evening the whole village came together for a feast. The women cooked all day, roasting pigs over glowing coals. Sarah helped by turning a spit, though she shuddered a little when she saw that the head had been left on.

The men did little but sit about and tell stories while the women hurried about doing all the cooking. They grilled fish over the coals and roasted a young deer, too, and it was quite a marvelous feast.

Jere sat beside the chief, while across from them sat Chan and the high priest. Sarah, standing with the women, noticed that Chan and Nomus were glowering.

More than once, Chan and Nomus glanced across the table and whispered to each other.

"What does she see in that puppy, Nomus?" Chan once grumbled.

The priest grinned evilly. "More than she sees in you, I think."

He knew that Chan was determined to have Lomeen for one of his wives. For some reason she seemed equally determined to have nothing to do with him.

"Let me catch him out alone sometime," Chan said. "We'll see what he can do."

Nomus turned sour. He did not like the way things were going, either. Somehow Chief Maroni had softened and mellowed under the influence of the young man and the Sleeper they called Sarah. He felt that his power over the chief was slipping away from him. But he would regain it. His mind worked constantly, trying to think of a way.

When most of the eating was over, and the men sat around drinking a brew that bit at Sarah's throat so that she would not try it again, Chief Maroni said, "Now we will have entertainment."

Jere turned to Lomeen, who was standing behind him. "Come and sit down, Lomeen. Let us watch the fun."

Lomeen looked nervously toward her father. "Our women do not sit in the presence of men."

Jere said. "It's the same with us, but I don't see why. I think that is rather silly."

"Good for you, Jere," Sarah whispered.

The chief had taken all this in. As the entertainment began, he questioned Jere about the customs of the Cloud People. He listened for a time, then said, "It is too bad that our tribes don't get along better."

"It is indeed a shame, Chief," Sarah said quickly from behind him, seeing her opportunity. "The two tribes could share so many things. The Cloud People could learn from you how to hunt better."

"Especially if we were allowed to get on the ground without getting killed," Jere said.

The chief blinked thoughtfully, but he said, "It is the way things are."

"It's the way things are, but it is not the way things have to be," Jere said. "See how well we're getting along here."

From across the table, Nomus gave the young stranger a hard glance. Then the high priest muttered to Chan, "I'll have to do something about this."

"Let me take care of him. I'll take him for a walk, and he'll never come back."

"No. That won't do." His eyes fell on the girl Sarah then, and an idea came to him. He said nothing more, but he stroked his cheek and let himself smile an evil smile.

Sarah enjoyed the simple entertainment—it was graceful folk dancing.

Jere too watched with a smile. When it was finished, he applauded, saying, "Wonderful! I wish I could dance like that!"

"What can you do to entertain us, Prince Jere?" Chief Maroni asked.

"Not much. I can tell a story perhaps."

"Good. We love stories here."

What followed next was very interesting to Sarah, watching from the cooking fire.

Jere came to his feet and soon proved to have the natural gift of a storyteller. His words were smooth and flowing, and especially since he was talking to people who could not read—whose only entertainment was oral stories—he was well received. Everyone grew quiet as he told of a great hunt in which a noble chief slew a mighty monster.

Maroni leaned forward, his face solemn and filled with interest as he listened. When Jere ended, he applauded wildly. "That was a fine story! Do you know any more?"

"Oh, I could go on forever," Jere said with a laugh. Then he told a funny story, which had all the villagers in an uproar.

Sarah went back to stand beside Lomeen. She saw that the girl's eyes were fixed on the young man. "He's a wonderful storyteller," Sarah said.

"Yes, and my father loves stories. So do I."

When the hour grew late, the chief dismissed everyone. As he prepared to go back to his house, he said to Lomeen, "Walk with me, daughter. That was a fine feast."

"Yes, it was."

"That young man. Jere. If he had any ambition, he'd be a great leader. Anyone who can tell stories like that can get people to do things. I've noticed that before. He has quite an imagination."

"Yes, he has."

Maroni looked down at her and smiled. "I notice you watched him quite a bit."

"He was very interesting."

"Nice looking, isn't he?"

"I hardly noticed."

Maroni laughed and patted his daughter on the shoulder. "I saw how you didn't notice. You didn't take your eyes off him."

"I wish," Lomeen said suddenly, "that we didn't have to slay any more of the Cloud People, Father. If they are all like Jere, to do so is a shame."

Maroni was thoughtful as they continued their

walk over the bridges. "I remember when your mother was alive. She knew some of the Cloud People. She liked them very much. Those I met, I liked, too. In fact, I knew King Celevorn when we both were young. He's a good man."

"Then why do we have to keep on killing them?"

Maroni had no answer. Actually he was troubled every time a sacrifice took place. Finally he said, "Nomus says that Nimbo demands sacrifice. And you wouldn't have us sacrifice our own people, would you?"

"I wouldn't have us sacrifice anybody!"

"You are not afraid of Nimbo? Not afraid that we will offend the god?"

"I don't think there is any Nimbo."

The chief was absolutely shocked. He stopped walking and turned to his daughter. "What are you saying, Lomeen?"

"I think the high priest uses that story about Nimbo just to get what he wants from us. Suppose there were no Nimbo. Would you honor Nomus the way you do?"

He supposed she saw the answer in his face.

"No, you wouldn't. You've never liked him, Father. But you're afraid of him."

Maroni did not like his daughter to think that he was afraid of anyone. "I am just afraid that bad things will happen to our people. That's why I listen to him."

"Another thing, Father," she said. "I don't want you to give me to Chan. He's a brutal man. I hate him."

"He wants you for his wife. He's the strongest man in the tribe."

"But he's awful!"

Maroni was even more troubled. Chan had been asking him for some time for his daughter. Knowing

Lomeen's feelings, he had refused so far. Now he saw the distress on her smooth face. He loved this daughter as he had loved her mother. He said, "Chan may change."

The day after the feast, the chief went on a hunt. He asked Jere and Sarah to go with him.

The three of them went far into the forest, and Sarah was amazed at the knowledge of Chief Maroni. He not only was an expert woodsman, but it seemed he knew every plant and every tree. He was also a very pleasant companion, something she had not imagined when she had first met him.

The hunt, however, was fruitless. In spite of Chief Maroni's skill, they could not stir up anything.

But when they were on their way home, a large deer suddenly appeared, and Maroni said, "What a beauty! But he is too far away."

Sarah measured the distance with her eye. Without a word, she slipped an arrow from her quiver and notched it.

"You could never hit him at this distance!" Chief Maroni protested.

Sarah did not say anything. She lifted the bow, judged the distance again, and drew back the string to a full draw. Holding her breath for a moment, she let it go. The arrow hissed through the air and struck the deer behind the shoulder.

"You've got him!" Jere shouted. "What a shot!"

"What a shot, indeed!" Maroni said, gaping at her. "I have never seen anything like that! None of our people could have done it. I myself could not have done it."

Sarah said quietly, "Perhaps it is because my bow is better. Would you like to look at it, Chief?"

Chief Maroni took the bow and examined it. It was a beautiful piece of work. And she had obviously discovered how to get maximum power from the wood. Maroni was impressed.

"It's a beautiful bow."

"I'd be glad to make you one just like it, Chief." Sarah had become an expert not only at using a bow but in making them.

"Would you, indeed? You can make bows? That would be a treasure!" the chief exclaimed.

Jere and the chief made a sling and carried the huge deer home.

There was much excitement in the village over their successful hunt, and that night Jere told, in poetic form, how Sarah had slain the deer.

It was another good evening until afterward. Nomus came to the chief and growled, "Things are not good, Chief Maroni."

"What are you talking about, Nomus?"

"Nimbo must be appeased. He needs a victim. He has not had one in a long time."

"But things are going well. None of our people are sick, the crops are good. I think we will not have another sacrifice."

Nomus' face grew evil, and he said shrilly, "You will see! A terrible thing will come upon our people if Nimbo has no sacrifice!"

But for the first time in years, Chief Maroni refused to listen to the high priest's demand. "No!" he said firmly. "We are not going to kill anybody else!"

Nomus glared. "You will be sorry!" he said. "You will find out that Nimbo is strong."

Lomeen and Sarah had heard all this, and as

114

Nomus stalked off, Lomeen whispered, "Good for you, Father."

"I think you did wisely, Chief," Sarah said. "Perhaps now we can begin to make peace between your tribe and the Cloud People."

Nomus, grunting crossly, went to his hut. It was a filthy place. He rummaged through his collection of herbs and spices and finally found one he knew to be deadly. He held it up before his eyes, pinched it, and ran a spoon through it, looking at the dark crystals.

"This will change your mind, Maroni."

His plan was simple. He would see that some of this was put in the chief's food. It would make him sick. "Not enough to kill him," he murmured. "Just enough to show him how strong Nimbo's power is." He laughed aloud. "Now we will see who dies."

12

Death to the Female

I can't understand, Sarah said to herself late one afternoon, *why I haven't heard anything from the Cloud People. Surely Josh and the others must have gotten to their village by now.*

She was walking along a stream, stopping from time to time to look down into the clear depths. She watched a group of silver-bodied minnows as they darted just below the surface. She wondered how they all knew what to do at the same time. "It's like they have one brain," she said. She had also wondered how birds knew how to keep perfect formations in the skies or how flights of blackbirds could all turn at the same time. "I guess the Creator just put it in them to know how to do those things," she murmured.

She moved along, thinking now of how she had come to admire Chief Maroni. He was a stern man in many ways, as any primitive tribesman would be, and yet he had true affection for all of his people. It was true that women were held in low esteem here. That was something that troubled her, and she remembered that it was the same with the Cloud People. She wondered if things could ever be any different, for habits were deeply ingrained.

The flowers were blooming. *It's beautiful here in a different way from the village in the clouds. Though that is beautiful, too.* Her thoughts went back to the village in the trees, and she wondered what Abbey was doing.

All morning she wandered by herself. Suddenly Sarah was lonely and somewhat afraid. *What if Josh and the others never find us? Sooner or later something's going to have to happen.*

When she got back to the village, she found Lomeen in front of the chief's house. "Hello, Lomeen," she said.

"Oh, Sarah, it's Father! He's very sick."

"What's wrong with him?"

"I don't know. It was after supper last night. The servants called me. He was crying out with pain."

"Oh my!" Sarah said. "That's terrible!"

"He *looks* terrible. Come and see him. Can you help?"

The chief did indeed look terrible. Standing beside his cot, she saw that his face was absolutely devoid of color. His lips were pale, and he moaned constantly, clutching his stomach.

"Do you know anything to do for him, Sarah?"

"I'm not a doctor," Sarah said. "Obviously something is wrong with his stomach. What did he eat last night?"

"The same as always. Some deer stew that I prepared for him myself."

"Did anyone else get sick?"

"No. No one." She thought for a moment , then said, "Nomus was here. He ate the same thing as my father."

"We'd better go find out if he's sick."

They did not have to go far. As soon as they stepped outside, Sarah saw Nomus himself standing there, an evil expression on his face. "I hear your father is sick," he said to Lomeen.

"He has a stomachache."

Sarah thought it quite clear that Lomeen did not like the high priest at all.

"I'll have to see him." Nomus brushed by the girl and glared at Sarah. He said nothing to her, however, but went in to stand over the chief, who opened his eyes but could only groan.

"Well, Chief, I am sorry to see you like this," Nomus said. His face turned grim. "But it is as I told you. Nimbo is angry."

"No. It's not that. I'll be all right."

"You will get worse, and you will die if Nimbo is not appeased."

Sarah cast a glance at Lomeen. It was not difficult to see where the high priest was going. He was going to demand a sacrifice. She thought she knew who the sacrifice would be—Jere or herself.

The chief listened as Nomus continued to tell him that the only way that he could live was to sacrifice a person to Nimbo.

Sarah was sure that ordinarily Chief Maroni would have agreed. But things seemed to have changed for him. Perhaps he had become fond of Jere in the few days the young man had been there. Perhaps he had seen in Sarah something he admired. In any case, he continued to shake his head, saying, "No. No sacrifice. I'll be all right."

Nomus glowered at him. "I will do the best I can for you, but I must be completely in charge of your case."

Both girls were put out of the chief's bedroom, and the rest of the day the high priest stayed with him. He finally came out to say, "Your father is going to die."

"No!" Lomeen cried. "He can't die!"

Sarah was fearing appendicitis and knew there

would be no cure for the chief in this society, for no one could perform that kind of operation. "I still hope that Goél will come, Lomeen. I've seen him do marvelous things for sick people."

"Goél," Nomus sneered. "He will not come."

It was indeed a faint hope, but it was all Sarah had to cling to.

Nomus was with the chief all night, but the next morning Lomeen's father was so feeble that he could barely speak. He seemed close to death.

Nomus announced, "You will die this day if there is not a sacrifice."

Sarah doubted that Maroni knew what the priest was saying. But he may have nodded, for Nomus cried out triumphantly, "Then I will attend to it!"

Sarah watched as Nomus left. "What's he going to do?"

Lomeen could barely answer. She was trying to hold back the tears. "He will choose a victim, and the victim will die."

By noon the whole village knew that there was going to be a sacrifice. People began gathering in the village square.

Nomus stood before them and said loudly, "The chief is very sick. He is about to die. It is because we have not sacrificed to Nimbo. The god is angry, but when he has his sacrifice, the chief will get well. I promise you."

Sarah looked around and saw fear on every face. "What will happen now, Lomeen?"

"Now Nomus will choose the victim."

Sarah could not imagine how even an evil man such as Nomus could simply select a victim to sacrifice. He did not look at her, but somehow Sarah sensed that she was in great danger.

The high priest said, "We will have the Test!"

"What's the Test?" Sarah whispered.

"Everyone must pass before Nomus and endure the Test by Water."

"What's that?"

"You will see. He does not often choose a victim this way."

Nomus ordered Chan to bring a huge stone basin and set it before him. He filled it with water. "The water is clear, as you see. If your heart is clear, you have nothing to be afraid of. The Test will now begin. You first, Lomeen, as the daughter of the chief."

Lomeen reluctantly went forward. She stood before Nomus and did not move.

"Put your hand in the water," he said.

Slowly Lomeen reached out and immersed her hand.

Nomus then seized her wrist. He held her hand high. "You see! Her hand is clean! She is not chosen by Nimbo!"

Sarah watched as one by one the villagers went through the same ceremony. Every person plunged his right hand into the water. Nomus took each one by the wrist and held up the hand, saying, "You have passed the Test by Water! Your heart is clean!"

Finally all the villagers had been tested, and Nomus pointed suddenly with a long, skinny finger. "Now, bring the Cloud person here."

Jere glanced at Sarah. He held his head high and went forward. Without waiting, he plunged his hand into the water. He looked straight at Nomus and said, "Do your worst, old man. I'm not afraid of you."

Nomus glared, but he pulled Jere's hand free and held it high. "You have passed the Test, Cloud Dweller." He then turned to Lomeen and said, "Bring the girl, the Sleeper."

Sarah went forward, somehow knowing what would happen.

She stood before Nomus and held his gaze. If she had ever seen pure evil in the eyes of a human being, it was in the eyes of the high priest.

"Now, Sleeper, we shall see if you have what you are."

"I'm not afraid of you, Nomus," Sarah said quietly.

The entire area had fallen quiet, for all seemed to know that the Test with Sarah was important.

"Put your hand in the water!"

Sarah put her hand in the water, and she saw Nomus reach forward. Something happened very quickly. The water turned red. The priest grasped her wrist and brought out her hand. It was stained as red as if plunged in blood. Sarah knew that Nomus had staged this. *He put something in the water!* she thought. But she had no time to protest.

"Her hand is red! She failed the Test of Water. Her heart is wrong. She is the victim for Nimbo."

"No!" Jere cried out.

Chan reached out and held the young man easily with his massive strength.

"Put her in hold. Nimbo now has a victim."

Sarah was dragged away and not allowed to speak. She caught a glimpse of Lomeen and saw the fear in the young girl's eyes.

She had no time to see more, however, because she was thrown into a rude hut. It was semidark inside. On the floor was a mat. There was no furniture at all, and she paced back and forth trying to conquer the panic that washed over her.

For a long time she walked, and then she took a deep breath. *I've been in worse places than this*, she thought. *Goél will not fail me.*

It was late that night when she heard a scratching at the door. She went to the hut entrance and heard a whispered voice.

"Sarah, are you awake?" It was Lomeen.

"Yes, I am, Lomeen."

"Jere is with me. Tell us what we can do."

"Can you get me out of here?"

"No. The guard has gone just for a minute. We can stay for only a few moments. Tell us what to do."

Sarah thought quickly. "You must go back to your village, Jere. My fellow Sleepers must be there by now. Go to Josh. Tell him what has happened."

"We will go at once," Jere said.

"Then we must go quickly," Lomeen whispered. "I fear the sacrifice will take place very soon."

Jere said, his voice harsh, "I'll bring my people. We'll save you, Sarah."

"Would you really bring your people to overthrow Nomus?" Lomeen asked as they turned away from the hut.

"It would be almost useless. My people are not trained as Chan has trained his men. But we will see. We must save Sarah."

Lomeen frowned. "I hesitate to leave my father . . ."

"You stay here. I will go for the Sleepers."

"No, I will go with you. Perhaps if you seem to have me as a hostage, your father will listen and be willing to help."

"If he does not, you and I will come back alone, Lomeen."

"Would you really do that?"

"Yes. I've become very fond of Sarah." He hesitated and said, "You remind me of her."

"Oh, I'm not nearly so pretty as she is."

Jere smiled. "That's your opinion," he said. "It's not mine. Now let us go for the Sleepers."

13

Time of the New Moon

There it is, Lomeen," Jere said. He stopped and pointed upward toward the tops of the magnificent trees that rose like towers before them. "What do you think of it?"

Lomeen had felt no fear as long as she was in the territory that her tribe inhabited. But the size of these trees somehow frightened her. She looked up at them, swallowed hard, then lowered her eyes.

"They make me dizzy just to look at them," she said.

"Really? I never thought about that. I guess it's all in the way you're brought up," Jere said with surprise. He studied her face, apparently finding it pleasing. "I never saw a woman that could keep up with me as well as you did," he commented. "As a matter of fact, I think perhaps you could outrun me down here on the ground."

Lomeen managed a smile. "I hope I'll do as well in your part of the world, but I have to tell you, Jere. I've always been a little afraid of heights." She shook her head at a faint childhood memory. "The other boys and girls could always climb trees better than I could."

"You don't have to be afraid in the trees. I'll hold you so that you won't fall."

"Will you?"

"Of course I will. And we'll be there soon."

The two continued their walk through the towering forest. The birds were so far overhead that Lomeen could hardly hear them. She had never been to this part of the woods before, although she had heard her father and other hunters tell of the Cloud People and the odd way they had of living. Now, as they passed among the huge, smooth tree trunks, she would venture a glance upward every now and then and wonder what in the world it would be like to live without touching the earth.

Lomeen had always loved the earth. The feel of the spring grass under her feet gave her delight. When the snow came, she liked to walk through it. But she knew there would be none of either in the village of the Cloud People. Silently she followed after Jere.

At last he stopped. "Here we are. And don't be afraid." He gave a piercing whistle that almost played a little tune. "That means 'Let the basket down.' We have a lot of signals. If you're going to stay with us, you'll have to learn to whistle."

"I could never whistle," Lomeen said. "I pucker and blow, but nothing comes out."

"That's all right. I'll give you whistling lessons."

Lomeen heard a sound, and she looked upward. There, descending from overhead, came two large baskets. She could not see the source of them because of the foliage. Then the baskets landed with a thump, and she gazed at them hard. "You want me to get in there?"

"I think you'd better. I'll ride up with you this time to show you how." He climbed into one basket , and Lomeen slowly got into the other. "Here we go," he said cheerfully. He gave another piercing blast, and the baskets abruptly jerked.

"Oh, we're going up!" she cried.

"Well, we can't go down," Jere joked. "Just relax and enjoy yourself. Perhaps you'd better not look down for a while. Just look up, and you'll see something you've never seen before."

Lomeen took his advice. Every time her basket jolted, she wanted to cry out. But she did not want him to see her fear, so she made herself look at the leaves and the tree limbs that stretched straight outward from the trunk. She saw that many limbs were as large as the trees in her homeland. They were inhabited by squirrels and birds, including many woodpeckers.

And then Jere was saying, "Look, Lomeen. You can see the platforms from here—and some houses."

Eagerly she looked upward. Sure enough, she saw platforms here and there along with simple buildings made of what looked like bamboo. She knew bamboo was lightweight, and she wondered at building houses out of such fragile material.

"Well, you're back at last."

The baskets came to a halt, and Jere jumped out. He greeted a youth standing on the platform, then turned and put out his hand. "Let me help you out."

She eagerly grasped his hand and stepped out of the basket. Then she made the mistake of looking down. The earth seemed so far away it made her gasp, and she swayed from side to side. Without meaning to, she fell against Jere with a gasp.

"That's all right. It gets to you a little bit if you're not used to high places," he said. "And, Lomeen, this is my friend Teanor."

"Where have you been, and where is the Sleeper?" the young man Teanor said with irritation.

"I've been visiting Chief Maroni. This is his daughter, Lomeen. Teanor is not one of the better looking of our people, but we put up with him just the same."

"Never mind my looks. Your father has been fright-

127

fully worried. You're going to have some explaining to do."

"I'll write a poem about it," Jere said. "As a matter of fact, I already have."

Throwing up his hands, Teanor said, "I don't want to hear any of your poetry. Tell me one thing. Please— did you see my brother while you were there?"

"I did, Teanor. I was able to visit him. They are keeping him a prisoner, but he's safe so far."

"Why didn't they release him and send him back with you?" Teanor cried.

"I can't explain all that to you just now. I must see my father first."

The trip to the king's house from the platform where she had gotten off the basket was terrifying to Lomeen. At first she clung to Jere, and he steadied her.

He kept making comforting sounds. "It's all right. You're not going to fall. You'll get used to it."

"I never will," she gasped.

However, even during the short time that it took to get to the palace, she found herself becoming some-what more accustomed to the high places. True enough, when they crossed the narrow, swaying bridges that connected the different platforms, she often closed her eyes, and Jere guided her across. But once her feet were on a solid platform, she began to find that it really was not so bad after all.

"You see. You're going to like it," Jere said. "Now I want you to meet my father."

They entered the tree palace, and Lomeen saw that every eye was upon Prince Jere. She supposed that everyone had been anxious about him.

King Celevorn was seated on his throne, and Lomeen got a good look at him. He gave her one flickering glance and then paid her no more attention. He gazed steadily at Jere and demanded, "Well, what do you have to say for yourself this time? What have you accomplished?"

"Father, I'm sorry I've disappointed you in the past," the prince said. "But I think you'll be glad to find out that I have some ideas about how our people can live from now on."

King Celevorn glared. "You never gave me a good idea in your life!" he said harshly. "All you've ever done is write poems, sing songs, and dance!"

The prince lowered his head for a moment, and Lomeen sensed that even the servants were waiting breathlessly.

Looking up, Jere said solemnly, "You're right, Father, and I want to do better. I've been lax in my duties to you and to our people, but that's going to be different from now on."

A light leaped into King Celevorn's eyes. "You mean you're giving up poetry?"

"I still think poetry is good, Father—as are many other things. But I want to do my best from now on to help our people, and I think I've found a way."

The king grunted. He suddenly turned to Lomeen. "And who is this female with you?"

"Sire, this is the daughter of Chief Maroni. Lomeen, this is my father, King Celevorn."

Lomeen bowed low and then straightened up. There was courage in her eyes, and she said clearly, "I am happy to meet you, O King."

"I am not happy to meet you nor any other Earth Dweller! Why did you bring *her* back here, Jere?"

At that moment there was a pounding of feet, and five young men and a girl rushed in. Suddenly the room seemed full. One of the newcomers cried, "We heard that your son has come back, Your Majesty!"

"Yes, friend Josh. This is my son, and this is a female he has brought from the land of the Earth Dwellers." He turned to the prince. "These are the servants of Goél who have come to help us."

"What did they say?" the one called Josh demanded. "What did the Earth Dwellers say about Sarah? Where is she?"

"I haven't had time to ask him. He's been making all kinds of promises about how he's going to be a better man than he has been up to now."

"I do hope to prove myself to you, Father. But let me tell you now what has happened. In the first place," he said, "the enemy is not Lomeen's father. Chief Maroni is a fine man. He says he met you once and that he liked you very much."

Celevorn shifted uncomfortably. "We did meet once when we were both very young, and I did like him. But that was before he started killing our people."

"It is not my father who does this," Lomeen spoke up, and everyone in the room seemed shocked that a mere female would speak in the presence of the king. "Your enemy is Nomus, the high priest."

"I have heard of him. Why do you say he is the enemy?" Apparently the king had decided to listen to her.

"Because," Lomeen said, "he has such an evil influence over my father. When my mother was alive there was none of this, if you will remember."

"I do remember. This trouble between us has come only recently, I'll admit. What about this Nomus?"

"And where is our friend Sarah?" the boy Josh demanded again. "Tell us that first."

"She's held prisoner, I'm afraid," Jere said. "She sent us back with a message to you, the Sleepers."

"What is it?" Josh eyes were bright with excitement.

"She said for me to tell you that she is prisoner and begs you to rescue her. At least that's what I think she meant."

"That is what she said, though not in exactly those words!" Lomeen exclaimed. "Please help us rescue her, Your Majesty."

"I promised her that, Father. We must take some of our people and save her. And Teanor's brother as well."

King Celevorn gaped at him as though the young man he was looking at was not his own son at all. But then he said, "How can we do that? We are very few, and they are many. And they are warriors."

"We must not fear, Father. Once we get rid of the evil influence of the priest, our people can work together. There will be no more captives, no more sacrifice."

King Celevorn continued to stare at his son. "I would like to believe you, but—"

"Your Majesty, I hope that you will send your people to save our companion, Sarah," Josh said quietly. Then he straightened and looked the king straight in the face. "But whether you send help or not, I must go and save her."

"So say we all," another Sleeper called out. And all the rest of the Sleepers nodded.

"And I promised that I would go back, Father," the prince said. "I do not want to displease you, but it is so important that we rescue Sarah at once. She will be sacrificed to that awful Nimbo if we do not."

"I—I will have to call the council together."

"There is not time for that, Father! Lomeen tells me that they sacrifice on the new moon, and that is tomorrow!"

An exclamation leaped to Josh's lips. "Tomorrow! Then we must go immediately!"

The Sleepers turned to leave the throne room, but the king arose and cried, "Stop!" He waited until they all faced him, and then he came down from the platform that the throne was set upon and put his hands on his son's shoulders. The prince had grown taller than he. He studied the young man's eyes and then said quietly, "My son, I have waited many years to see any sign of the ruler in you and have seen none. I do not know what you have gone through with the Earth Dwellers, but something has changed you."

"I think he has become a man, Your Majesty," Lomeen said.

The king turned to her. He smiled briefly. "You remind me of his mother. She was always outspoken."

Lomeen found herself liking King Celevorn. "I must warn you that a rescue effort will be dangerous, Your Majesty. Nomus is an evil man, and Chan is the chief of warriors. If, somehow, those two could be removed, there would be no trouble at all between our people. We can learn much from each other."

Still King Celevorn hesitated. It was probably hard to order men into danger when he knew full well that some might not return. But then, looking into the clear eyes of the prince and lifting his voice, he said, "We will go. Get your weapons and let us make ready."

"Now—" Jere turned back to Lomeen "—I must warn you that it will be dangerous not only for us but for your friends and your family."

"I know, but something must be done to stop Nomus."

Jere looked at her fondly. "Well, we will do the best we can to resolve this with as little injury to anyone as possible."

"Be very careful, Jere," Lomeen said quickly. She lowered her eyes.

He reached out and took her hand. "We will talk more later. Now it is time to go to war."

Sarah heard the heavy bar being drawn away from the door of her prison, and she came to her feet. She no sooner was standing than Chief Maroni himself entered. His face was thin from his illness, but she was delighted to see him now able to walk about. She told him so.

But he asked at once, "Are you being well treated?"

"I have food and water and a place to sleep."

Maroni noted the brevity of her answer. He shook his head sadly. "I'm sorry all this happened."

"So am I," Sarah said. "And it doesn't have to happen."

Maroni began to pace about the hut. "I am the chief, but you must understand that my powers are limited by—" He stopped pacing then and stood looking down at her. He was a tall man and strong, though age was beginning to mark him. "I am confused," he murmured, and his eyes were troubled. He looked away and said, "Frankly, I do not know what to do."

"I believe you do know, Chief Maroni," Sarah said quietly.

Maroni looked back at her with astonishment.

"I think most of the time people know what is the right thing to do. It's finding the courage to do the right thing that gives us problems."

"You speak very firmly for so young a female."

"Doing the right thing is not a matter of being old or young, is it, Chief?"

Maroni did not answer this. Obviously, he knew she spoke the truth.

He chewed on his lip and then said mournfully, "I wish my wife was alive."

"Lomeen's mother."

"Yes. I never saw anybody as wise as she was. Of course, she was very quiet, and people did not know her as I did." A thoughtful expression crossed his face, and he said, "Looking back, I believe that many of the good decisions I made came from her, a female!"

"She sounds like a wonderful woman."

"Yes, she was a female, but somehow she was able to think things through. I was always too impulsive, Sarah. Many times she kept me from acts that would have been very bad indeed."

"And what do you think she would want you to do in this matter of sacrificing to Nimbo?"

Chief Maroni smote his forehead with his hand and said angrily, "That is what I have been asking myself."

"And I think you know the answer," Sarah repeated.

She saw that Chief Maroni was in an agony of grief. The daughter whom he loved more than anything else in his kingdom was gone. Thoughts of his dead wife tormented him. Now he drew himself up to his full height. "I think you are right," he said finally.

"May I say one more word to you, Chief?"

"Of course."

"I think you also need to be more considerate of the females of your tribe."

"That is what my wife always said," he admitted.

"I don't personally mistreat females, though. You know that."

"But you see them as nothing but servants, and they're more than that. Remember the wisdom of your wife."

"Why do you say this to me?"

"Because I think it is what your wife probably said to you, and you didn't listen." Suddenly Sarah was convinced that if she could get the idea of the value of girls and women into the chief's mind, her mission would be fulfilled no matter what happened to her tomorrow. "I hope you will consider what I've said, Chief. I think it would make you and your men better persons if you treated your wives as well as you treat each other."

Chief Maroni seemed to think long and hard. He drew his shoulders together and then allowed them to slump. "You are wise, just like my wife," he said. "All the time you were talking, I was remembering that she said almost the same things. However—" he sighed "—unfortunately we have other things before us just now. Things that affect you."

"And you mean Nomus and what he wants to do to me."

"As I said, though I am chief, my power is limited. The high priest has bought the loyalty of Chan and all the warriors. And if I try to cross Nomus . . ."

"You mean they would listen to him before they would listen to you?"

Chief Maroni looked away. "I fear so, though it is impossible to say. But I can see one thing. I have allowed the kingdom to slip away, and I am determined to get it back."

14

A Prince Becomes a Man

I just don't know if it can be done," Josh said doubtfully. He scratched his head and looked thoughtfully
around the circle, as his five companions studied his
face. Josh felt uncertain about the entire rescue mission
and had found it better to be truthful with the others.

"What's the matter, Josh?" Jake asked. "We've han-
dled tougher things than this."

"We don't really know that, Jake," Josh answered
quickly. "We don't know what we're running into exactly."

Reb grinned. "It won't be T-rexes, at least. The
Earth Dwellers couldn't have anything that bad."

Josh well remembered the time the Sleepers had
been forced to battle awful monsters with six-inch
teeth like chisels. "What bothers me," he said, "is that
the Cloud People are very peaceable. They don't know
anything about war or weapons, really. They've led
very sheltered lives."

"You're right about that," Prince Jere said, and his
brow furrowed. He and Lomeen had both been invited
to sit in on the Sleepers' council. "And I'll have to add,
Josh, that the Earth Dwellers have become a fierce
people."

"And that does make things a little tough," Dave
Cooper put in. "Is there any chance we can sneak in
and get Sarah away without being seen?"

"I wouldn't think so," Jere said, "now that Nomus
knows there are more Sleepers. He'll expect a rescue
attempt."

"Jere is right," Lomeen said. And since she knew the Earth Dwellers better than anyone else, all gave her their close attention. "Naturally, the victims chosen for sacrifice are determined to get away, so Chan puts an extra heavy guard around them."

"What about this fellow Chan?" Wash said. "Is he a pretty tough cookie?"

"Chan is a very brutal, vicious man," Lomeen said.

"And that's why she didn't want to be his wife," Jere said.

Lomeen's face flushed. "That is reason enough. He is cruel and vicious, and he'll stop at nothing to get his own way. If it wasn't for Chan and the warriors, the priest wouldn't be able to wield so much influence over my father."

"Then maybe what we ought to do," Josh said slowly, "is go in and try to get rid of Chan. Perhaps that would discourage his warriors into surrendering."

"You would have trouble doing that," Lomeen said. "He is always surrounded by his guards."

The talk went around the circle until finally Josh said, "We don't have much time left. We've got to leave soon."

"I agree," Jere said. "And another problem is getting close without being seen."

"Does Chan have scouts out, Lomeen?" Abbey asked.

"Usually he does," she said slowly, "though there won't be so many just now."

"Why not?"

"Because the scouts are all interested in being at the sacrifice. As I said, they are cruel men, and they wouldn't want to miss an event like this."

Josh shrugged his shoulders. "Well, we'll just have

to go and play it by ear and count on Goél's help. I say what we do is hit the village and just try to take Sarah out of danger. Never mind fighting anybody."

"You won't rescue Sarah without taking on Chan and his guards," Lomeen said firmly.

"Then we'll take him on if we have to. Let's get our weapons together and gather the men who've offered to accompany us. We'll need to go over our tactics with them."

Teaching the Cloud People to fight was a task that would have taken more time than Josh and the Sleepers had. But the people were willing enough, and Josh did discover one good thing about them.

"They're the *quickest* people I ever saw," he said.

"That comes from living in the trees," Jere said. "You've got to be quick and sure if you want to live here. And then, of course, climbing up and down gives you strength."

"Some of them are good archers as well," Celevorn said. The king had joined his son and the Sleepers as they tried to instill some sort of order on the men who would travel with them.

The Earth Dwellers will overwhelm these smaller people if it comes to a matter of battle with staves and swords, Josh thought. That there were some good archers was their only hope. Unfortunately, the best archer among the Sleepers was Sarah, and she would not be available.

Celevorn watched Josh explain his plan of attack. He also watched his son, who seemed eager to take part. He murmured to Lomeen, "I don't know what you've done to my son, but he seems to have become a man indeed."

"He's a very fine man, Your Majesty," Lomeen answered quickly. "He doesn't have to go back to my village, and he didn't have to go there in the first place. I admire him a great deal."

The king studied her slyly. "I can see that you do." He saw the blush mount in her cheeks and laughed. "That's all right. I am glad you like him. And I can see that he likes you, too."

"Now, listen," Josh said. "Here's what we'll have to do. We've got to get to the village without being seen. If we try to go in a body, there's a good chance that one of Chan's lookouts will see us. Would it be possible for us to break up into very small groups—no more than three or four—and come at the village from different directions?"

"That will work," Jere said quickly. "We can arrange a meeting point. What do you think would be a good place, Lomeen?"

The men among the Cloud People looked shocked. To ask a female's advice about such an important matter was probably unheard of.

Lomeen said, "We could all meet at the thick woods just north of the village. Then the attack could be made directly in force."

"I'm hoping that we can hit them hard enough and quick enough that they'll surrender," Jere said. "I intend to go for Chan, and if I can take him out, the others will be more likely to give up."

"He is a mighty warrior," Lomeen said nervously.

"And I'm a mighty maker of poems, so we'll see who comes out on top."

As they were about to leave for the rescue, King Celevorn took Josh aside. "No matter what comes of this, it has been wonderful to see Prince Jere come to himself."

"I guess sometimes it takes a kind of crisis to bring young fellows out of their childhood, Your Majesty."

"I've always known there was good material in my son, but now I see it. And it's making me very proud." Abbey, standing beside Josh, was listening. "What would you think if your son wanted to marry Lomeen?" It was just the sort of question Abbey would ask, Josh thought.

"I think she's a fine young woman. There would be many problems to work out between our tribes, however."

"Back in OldWorld," Josh said, "sometimes kings and queens worked out their problems by arranging a marriage between a prince of one kingdom and a princess of another. That tied the two kingdoms together."

The thought seemed to interest King Celevorn, but there was no time to talk of it. The hour was growing late.

"Let's go," Josh said. "We've made all the plans we can, and now we've got to carry them out."

Vines were let down to the ground, and the Cloud People began descending from their homes high in the trees. Jere slid down easily, followed by Teanor and the others.

In the end, even King Celevorn had insisted on going along. "I'm not too old for this venture," he said. "I pulled a good bow in my youth, and now we'll see." He also had a sword at his side, which gleamed in the light as he held it up. "This will be the Cloud People's greatest battle."

The Sleepers seemed rather embarrassed about having to be let down in baskets. But Lomeen said to

Abbey, "It's scary being that high in the air. Still, I rather like it."

Hanging onto the side of her basket, Abbey grinned. "Good. You may be spending a lot of time up there," she said.

"Why would you say that?"

"I think you know."

Lomeen gave her a hard look but then giggled. "I don't know what you're talking about," she said.

When they were all on the ground, the king said, "Lomeen, I will ask you to be in my party along with my son. The rest, friend Josh, you will arrange."

And so the Sleepers were divided up with guides. The Cloud People began to lead them silently through the trees toward Sarah's rescue.

Nomus had asked for a conference with Chan. The two men were talking in front of the hut where the Sleeper Sarah was held captive.

"Make sure she doesn't get away, Chan," Nomus instructed.

"When was the last time anyone got away from *me?*" Chan boasted. "Don't worry about that."

"I wish the prince of the Cloud People hadn't gotten away. I'd like to see him put to death along with this female."

"Don't worry about that. After this is over, we shall make a raid. We'll catch him again."

"Be sure that you do." Nomus unbarred the door. He drew a knife as he stepped inside and looked at the prisoner with an evil grin. "This is your last day on earth. How does it feel, Sleeper?"

Sarah stood with her back to the wall, staring at

the priest. She was determined to show no fear of the man. "You're an evil man, Nomus," she said, "but your days are numbered."

"*My* days are numbered! That's a joke! You are the one who is going to die."

Sarah did not answer. She had faced death before in the Sleepers' many missions for Goél. Besides, she knew it would be shameful to show any sort of fear. She stood resolutely while Nomus taunted her.

The high priest stepped toward her, holding out his knife. "I could cut your throat even now," he said, "but I would rather wait and do it in public." He reached out suddenly and slapped her.

Sarah's face burned, but she said not a word.

Nomus threw the heavy bar against the door of the prison hut. "Put a double guard on her!" He scowled. "I don't want anything to happen. It will be quite a spectacle."

"I fear the chief is getting out of hand," Chan muttered. "You shouldn't have let him recover."

"Don't worry. *I'll* handle him. You do your job, and I'll do mine. We'll get rid of these Sleepers first, one at a time if we have to, and then we'll take care of the Cloud People. *Then*—" he grinned "—we might have a new chief of the Earth Dwellers."

Chan knew exactly what the high priest planned to do. "I would make a good chief, wouldn't I?"

"Yes, as long as you listen to someone with sense."

"Like you, Nomus?"

"Like me. You do the muscle work, and I'll do the thinking."

15

A Friend in the Darkness

Chief Maroni had come for a last visit with Sarah. In the midst of their talking, he abruptly muttered, "I haven't slept a wink since Lomeen left. Why would she leave me?"

Sarah was very much aware that the hour of her sentence was close. Nevertheless, she felt compassion for Maroni. She saw that he was still in poor physical condition. She had felt at first that he was just weak to allow himself to be ruled by Nomus and bullied by Chan, but now she sensed that basically he was a decent man. She said quietly, "I'm glad to see you have such love for your daughter, Chief."

"I didn't know how much I cared for her. If I could only get her back, things would be different."

"Different how, Chief?"

"For one thing I've been thinking of what you said about treating females better. I have not been cruel, but neither have I been kind or fair. If I just had time, I could show Lomeen how much I think of her. And not just her but the other women of the tribe as well."

"I'm so glad to hear you say that, Chief!" Sarah exclaimed. "It would make all the difference in the world. Not just to the women but to the men too."

"How do you see that?"

"I think that the women would be very grateful, but also they could be much more help to you than they have been. They are capable of doing more than simply washing clothes and cooking."

"Yes, I found that out with Lona, my wife." Then Maroni said, "And in the morning I'm going to have a talk with Nomus."

"About what he's going to do with me?"

"Yes. Of course."

"You may as well save your breath, Chief. He's determined to offer me as a sacrifice."

Maroni straightened up. He was a strong-willed man, though not young any longer. "We will see who is chief of the Earth Dwellers."

Maroni left, and the night wore on. Sarah was fairly certain that dawn would be the hour of the sacrifice. She remembered Lomeen's speaking of that hour to her. For a long time she paced back and forth. At last she sat down on the pad that she used for a mattress. Her back was against the wall, and to her amazement she began to doze off.

Sarah awoke with a start to find that she had been dreaming of her days as a Sleeper. She and her friends had experienced so many adventures, she thought. And suddenly she realized something. *If I had not been saved from that great nuclear war in OldWorld, I would have missed a lot. NuWorld has been hard and dangerous, but we've been able to serve Goél. And I've made such good friends here!*

For a long time she lay there half-asleep, thinking of all the people that she had met. Some of them had been strange indeed. Many had become fine friends— better than she could have imagined.

Then she nodded off and began dreaming again. This time she seemed to be in an even darker place than her small prison. Panic, like a raving beast, was trying to take over her heart. Sarah had known fear before but nothing like this. This was a nightmare such as she had never had, and she knew that she was screaming.

"Sarah, do not be afraid."

Sarah, in her dream, suddenly recognized the voice of Goél!

"Goél, is that you?"

"It is I. This is a difficult time for you," the voice went on quietly, "but I will be with you. Even though the knife is raised to plunge into your heart, do not fear."

Sarah felt the terror ebbing away. Soon it had disappeared entirely, and she whispered, "Goél?"

Then she knew she was awake.

"It was only a dream," she said with disappointment. But though it had been a dream, she felt new confidence. She got up and waited for the dawn with renewed hope. "I don't know what will happen, but Goél has never failed me," she said aloud. "He won't this time."

Her voice sounded thin and feeble, but somehow she knew that she had been visited by her friend Goél himself.

16

A New Way

All in the Earth Dwellers' village had gathered for the sacrifice. They came reluctantly, because most of them looked forward to it with nothing but dread. Nomus, however, had commanded Chan to see that every member of the tribe was there, and now they were met in the open space just outside the village. Thick trees formed a circle around the area, forming a natural amphitheater.

The high priest looked with satisfaction at Chan and said, "We'll put on a fine show today. It will bring the chief into line."

Chan grinned. "Shall I bring out the female now?"

"Yes. It is time."

The day had dawned red, and as Sarah stepped out of the hut at the command of Chan, she blinked at the brightness of the sky.

"A fine day to die, wouldn't you say?" The warrior grinned and grabbed her arm.

"Let go of my arm," Sarah ordered.

Chan blinked. He actually stepped back, releasing her. He no doubt was not accustomed to his victims' showing this kind of spirit. "We'll see how long you keep that up," he said. "When you see the knife, you'll scream like a wounded animal."

Sarah did not answer him. Now she was flanked on each side by guards, and one followed behind. Chan led the way. As they made their way through the village, she determined to show no sign of fear.

When she stepped out into the clearing, Sarah saw the evil form of Nomus at once. He was wearing a scarlet robe and had in his hand a wicked looking knife with a curved blade. Before him a stone rose out of the ground, huge and dark. There were stains on it, she saw, and she knew at once that they were bloodstains from earlier victims.

She passed along the ranks of villagers and saw pity in the eyes of most. Perhaps many had lost members of their own families to the cruel tactics of Nomus and his god. Although she was headed for her death, Sarah could not help but think, *There are enough men here to have a revolt if they just had a leader.*

Then she was brought to a halt before the great stone.

Nomus said, "You are a troublemaker, and this is the end of your trouble, Sleeper!" He held up the wicked knife to the crowd. "Nimbo must have a victim, and the chief nearly died because of this female," he shouted.

"That is not so!"

The villagers looked about for the speaker, and Sarah saw that it was none other than Chief Maroni himself. He wore the deep purple royal robe reserved for ceremonies. On his head he wore a headdress made from the feathers of exotic birds. Strapped on his side was a sword with a golden hilt, and now he laid his hand on it as he took his stand beside Sarah.

"There will be no sacrifice, Nomus."

A pleased murmur went up from the crowd.

Instantly Nomus cried, "The chief is beside himself! He is still not well! Take him away! Be gentle. I must treat him."

Maroni drew the sword with the golden hilt.

Before the chief could use it, though, Chan suddenly put his massive arms around him. Another guard removed the sword, and Maroni struggled helplessly. The sickness had apparently taken all of his strength, and he was easily carried away in the mighty arms of Chan.

Sarah had known a moment of hope, but now it was gone. As she saw Maroni being carried off, she cried loudly, "Earth Dwellers, do not let that beast misuse your king! Rise up!"

"Weapons out!" Nomus commanded the guards. "Slay any man who tries to stop the sacrifice!"

Sarah knew then that it was too late to organize a revolt. *I should have done it before*, she thought. *Why didn't I think of it?*

The evil voice of Nomus screeched, "Tie her to the stone!" and guards seized her arms.

Sarah was thrown upon the altar, where she lay facing the sky. It was blue and beautiful with white clouds drifting along. *The last sky I'll ever see*, she thought. They bound her with ropes then, and she could not move.

"Now you will see the power of Nimbo!" the priest cried. He stood over the helpless girl and grinned evilly into her face. "Are you ready to die?"

"I will always be ready to die to stand against evil such as you," Sarah said in a loud voice. "Earth Dwellers, you see what kind of man this is! When I die, do not let him control your lives!"

"Be quiet!" Nomus screamed. "I will hear no more." He raised the knife and shouted, "Now, Nimbo, here is your sacrifice!"

Sarah did not close her eyes. The bright edge of the knife caught the reflection of the sun, and she saw it poised over her heart. She knew that Nomus would have no pity, and she whispered, "Goél, I did my best! And you said not to fear."

The knife, however, did not descend. At that moment a feathered shaft pierced Nomus's wrist, and the sacrificial knife fell.

Then Sarah heard the voice that she knew to be Josh's shouting, "Sleepers, Cloud People—attack!"

"Josh, you're here!" she cried.

The Sleepers and the Cloud People fell upon Chan's guards with all the force they had. The arrows flew thick, but—according to Josh's instruction—only the guards were hit. The warriors tried to organize, but they could not match the onslaught of arrows.

"Follow me!" Chan roared. "These Cloud People can't fight!"

He rushed forward to lead the charge, but suddenly a figure appeared before him.

Turning her head, Sarah saw that it was Jere. He carried a sword in his hand.

"Surrender, Chan," Jere cried. "Surrender, and you will not be harmed."

Chan seemed unable to believe that this mere youth had challenged him. Raising his sword high, the warrior ran straight at him. "I'll kill you, and then I'll kill all of your people!" he bellowed. He swung his huge broadsword back and forth.

Jere ducked under the blade. It came so close to his head that he surely heard its hiss and felt it tugging at his hair. Then, without hesitation, he lunged toward

Chan. His sword was not long nor was it heavy, but it was keen.

Sarah saw Chan fall forward.

"Chan is dead! Surrender!" Prince Jere shouted.

Surrender came quickly when the guards saw that their leader was gone and that there was no hope.

And then Sarah looked up and saw Josh's face.

"Are you all right, Sarah?"

"Yes, Josh. I'm all right," she whispered.

"Let me cut those ropes."

Swiftly he cut her free and helped her sit up just in time to see that there was yet another crisis. King Celevorn was facing Chief Maroni.

"Look," Josh said. "I think those two have something to talk about."

Indeed they did. Celevorn bowed slightly. His sword was in his hand although he seemed not to have used it. "It has been a long time, Maroni."

"Yes, Celevorn," the chief said. "It has."

"The last years have been unhappy ones. You have been the enemy of my people."

"But no more," Lomeen said. She hurried to support her father, whose face was pale with weakness. "And it was not my father who was the enemy, but Nomus." She looked at the high priest.

Nomus was holding his bleeding arm, and his face was ashen.

"There is the source of all our troubles."

"You are right, my daughter. But I have been wrong, also," Maroni said quietly. "I ask your pardon, Celevorn, and the pardon of all of your people for the trouble that has been between us. As chief, I must stand responsible. But I say this—you will have no more problem with the Earth Dwellers."

153

Suddenly Prince Jere was standing beside Lomeen. The eyes of the two fathers then met, and a message seemed to pass between them.

A smile came to the face of the king as he replaced his sword. "We have much to talk about," he said.

"I must tell you, King Celevorn," Chief Maroni said, "that through all of this I have changed my opinion of females somewhat. I see them now in a higher light than I did before. As a matter of fact, may they not be the equal of men?"

But Celevorn was looking at his son. And Jere, who had put one arm around Lomeen, was watching him. "Well," the king said, stroking his chin, "that is indeed something else to talk about. But I think I know what you mean by that. I have been much impressed with your daughter. If all females are as wise and courageous as she, then we have been missing something."

"Isn't that sweet?" Abbey said. She had been fussing over Sarah. "I know what will happen now."

"What?" Sarah asked.

"They'll get married and live happily ever after."

"I doubt that," Josh grunted. "They'll get married and have arguments and have to learn to live together."

"Josh Adams, I keep telling you, you don't have a romantic bone in your body," Sarah snapped.

"Who, me? I'm very romantic."

"Why don't you ever write a poem—like Jere does?"

Josh suddenly grinned. "I know. I'll hire Jere to write me some poems. What would you like for them to say?"

"Oh, you're impossible!"

However, she saw later that Josh actually did go over to congratulate Jere. She also heard him say, rather uncomfortably, "Jere, is it hard to write a poem?"

Jere glanced at Sarah and saw that she was watching. He said, "Nothing to it. I'll teach you how."

"It seems that we're always solving problems and then leaving," Josh said. He and Sarah were helping each other adjust their knapsacks. "Just great problem solvers. That's us."

"But Goél used the Sleepers to do so much good here," Sarah said. "Both King Celevorn and Chief Maroni are agreed that things are going to be different. Any prisoners will be freed. And I suppose you noticed that the women sat right down with the men at our farewell banquet."

"Next thing you know they'll teach them to count money," Josh said with a straight face.

"Josh, you're truly impossible!" But she saw that he was smiling at her.

"Sarah, I want to tell you I was scared to death when you were in the hands of that monster Nomus."

"He is a monster, isn't he? What do you think will happen to him?"

"If there is any justice, he'll take your place on that altar. But I think he'll be taken care of. Maroni won't let him get off scot-free."

The two walked along slowly, and overhead a bird was singing. Josh glanced up at it. Then Sarah said, "Josh—"

"What?"

"I was wrong about the way I acted. I'm sorry."

Josh turned to her. "Thanks for the apology, but I was as wrong as you were, so let's forgive each other."

"And never do it again!" she exclaimed, smiling.

"Well, I think we ought to have a fight at least once a month."

"What!"

"Because it's kind of fun to make up." He reached over and gave her a squeeze. "There. And now I've got a little poem I'd like to read to you." He brought a piece of paper out of his pocket.

"Josh Adams, Jere wrote that poem," Sarah accused.

"He did not! He just gave me a few pointers. Now, here it is."

Josh read the poem, and Sarah listened. It was a terrible poem. But when he finished, she threw her arms around his neck and said, "Oh, Josh, that's the most beautiful poem I ever heard in my whole life!"

Get swept away in the many Gilbert Morris Adventures available from Moody Press:

"Too Smart" Jones

4025-8 Pool Party Thief
4026-6 Buried Jewels
4027-4 Disappearing Dogs
4028-2 Dangerous Woman
4029-0 Stranger in the Cave
4030-4 Cat's Secret
4031-2 Stolen Bicycle
4032-0 Wilderness Mystery
4033-9 Spooky Mansion
4034-7 Mysterious Artist

Come along for the adventures and mysteries Juliet "Too Smart" Jones always manages to find. She and her other homeschool friends solve these great adventures and learn biblical truths along the way. Ages 9-14

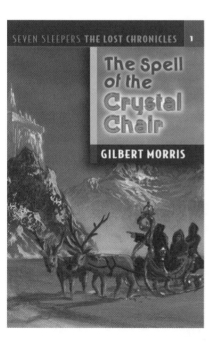

Seven Sleepers - The Lost Chronicles

3667-6 The Spell of the Crystal Chair
3668-4 The Savage Game of Lord Zarak
3669-2 The Strange Creatures of Dr. Korbo
3670-6 City of the Cyborgs
3671-4 The Temptations of Pleasure Island
3672-2 Victims of Nimbo
3672-0 The Terrible Beast of Zor

More exciting adventures from the Seven Sleepers. As these exciting young people attempt to faithfully follow Goél, they learn important moral and spiritual lessons. Come along with them as they encounter danger, intrigue, and mystery. Ages 10-14

Dixie Morris Animal Adventures

3363-4 Dixie and Jumbo
3364-2 Dixie and Stripes
3365-0 Dixie and Dolly
3366-9 Dixie and Sandy
3367-7 Dixie and Ivan
3368-5 Dixie and Bandit
3369-3 Dixie and Champ
3370-7 Dixie and Perry
3371-5 Dixie and Blizzard
3382-3 Dixie and Flash

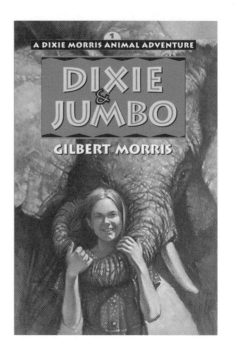

Follow the exciting adventures of this animal lover as she learns more of God and His character through her many adventures underneath the Big Top. Ages 9-14

The Daystar Voyages

4102-X Secret of the Planet Makon
4106-8 Wizards of the Galaxy
4107-6 Escape From the Red Comet
4108-4 Dark Spell Over Morlandria
4109-2 Revenge of the Space Pirates
4110-6 Invasion of the Killer Locusts
4111-4 Dangers of the Rainbow Nebula
4112-2 The Frozen Space Pilot
4113-0 White Dragon of Sharnu
4114-9 Attack of the Denebian Starship

Join the crew of the Daystar as they traverse the wide expanse of space. Adventure and danger abound, but they learn time and again that God is truly the Master of the Universe. Ages 10-14

MOODY
The Name You Can Trust
1-800-678-8812 www.MoodyPress.org

Seven Sleepers Series

3681-1 Flight of the Eagles
3682-X The Gates of Neptune
3683-3 The Swords of Camelot
3684-6 The Caves That Time Forgot
3685-4 Winged Riders of the Desert
3686-2 Empress of the Underworld
3687-0 Voyage of the Dolphin
3691-9 Attack of the Amazons
3692-7 Escape with the Dream Maker
3693-5 The Final Kingdom

Go with Josh and his friends as they are sent by Goél, their spiritual leader, on dangerous and challenging voyages to conquer the forces of darkness in the new world. Ages 10-14

Bonnets and Bugles Series

0911-3 Drummer Boy at Bull Run
0912-1 Yankee Bells in Dixie
0913-X The Secret of Richmond Manor
0914-8 The Soldier Boy's Discovery
0915-6 Blockade Runner
0916-4 The Gallant Boys of Gettysburg
0917-2 The Battle of Lookout Mountain
0918-0 Encounter at Cold Harbor
0919-9 Fire Over Atlanta
0920-2 Bring the Boys Home

Follow good friends Leah Carter and Jeff Majors as they experience danger, intrigue, compassion, and love in these civil war adventures. Ages 10-14

MOODY
The Name You Can Trust
1-800-678-8812 www.MoodyPress.org